# GUILTY AS SIN

## SIN TRILOGY BOOK TWO

# MEGHAN

*NEW YORK TIMES* BESTSELLING AUTHOR

# MARCH

# CONTENTS

# GUILTY AS SIN

Book Two of the Sin Trilogy

Meghan March

Visit my website at www.meghanmarch.com

Guilty until proven innocent.

That's the way the world works, right?

I'm tired of being convicted without evidence, all because my last name is Gable.

The Riscoffs might own this town, but I'm done following their rules.

If only I could forget just how easily Lincoln Riscoff can drag me under his spell.

*Guilty as Sin* is the second book in the Sin Trilogy.

# WHITNEY

*Ten years ago*

I RODE to the hospital with Aunt Jackie, shivering in my rain-soaked clothes as my stomach twisted into tighter and tighter knots. She wouldn't tell me anything other than there had been an accident involving my parents and Lincoln's father.

I glanced in the rearview mirror and saw Lincoln's headlights shining behind us. As soon as Jackie had given us the news, part of me had wanted to run to him, to give and seek comfort, but what had happened earlier tonight had changed everything between us. Although, the closer we got to the hospital, the less some stupid fight and angry words seemed to matter.

*There's nothing like a possible tragedy to force you to wake up and realize what matters. Life is precious. Tomorrow carries no guarantee.*

"What happened?" I felt like I'd asked the question a

thousand times, but Jackie had only given me the bare minimum in details.

My aunt glanced over at me for a second before training her eyes back on the road. The windshield wipers worked overtime on their highest setting, but she still had to squint to see through the downpour.

"I don't know. They wouldn't tell me much over the phone."

The knot in my stomach yanked tighter again, and I wrapped my arms around my middle as I shivered. "Why did they call you and not me?"

"I called you the entire way to your house, and it went straight to voice mail every time. They probably couldn't get through to you either."

"Oh my God. My phone was off," I whispered. "Because . . ."

Jackie's gaze cut to me again, but she didn't say anything.

Guilt savaged me. *I turned my phone off, and my parents were . . .*

I shook harder. "I would know if something really, really bad happened, wouldn't I? Shouldn't I feel something? Know something? They have to be okay, don't they?"

"Keep it together, Whit. We're almost there." Jackie's voice, normally so strong and confident, sounded as ragged as mine.

I checked the sideview mirror again because it gave me something to do. Anything was better than dwelling on the horrible possibilities flipping through my brain.

I forced myself to focus on the headlights behind us.

Lincoln's headlights. He'd come to my house, even after he'd thrown me out of the cabin, and I didn't know why. I thought he'd said everything he needed to say.

*Not that any of it matters now.* Because my parents and his father were in some kind of accident. *Together.*

Jackie guided the car into the parking lot of the Riscoff Memorial Hospital and took a spot about a hundred yards from the emergency entrance. Lincoln drove right up to the ER doors and jumped out. He stood beside his truck, staring in my direction.

As soon as Jackie shifted into park, I bolted out of the car and ran. Rain drenched my clothes, but I didn't care.

*I need to know.*

"Whit, wait!" Jackie yelled, but I didn't listen.

My brain buzzed with static and only one thought— *find out what's going on as quickly as possible.*

Lincoln met me as the automatic doors slid open. He reached out and grabbed my hand, interlacing his fingers with mine. "I don't give a shit what happened earlier. I'm not letting you face this alone. I don't give a damn what anyone says, including you."

All the anger I'd been harboring from our fight had already been obliterated by fear. My head bobbed a few times, but I couldn't find any words to reply.

He squeezed my hand, and I found a tiny measure of calm in the riot of emotions pummeling me.

Together, we walked through the doors and into the emergency room lobby. Everything was so white and bright, at complete odds with the storm raging outside.

As soon as the woman at the triage desk saw us, her face paled. "Mr. Riscoff, your family just arrived. They're

3

waiting for you in a private room, sir." Her gaze shifted to me, but it was clear she had no idea who I was.

"My parents were in the accident too. The Gables."

Lincoln squeezed my hand again as Jackie slid to a halt behind me, her shoes squeaking on the wet floor.

The woman's gaze cut from my face to Lincoln's and back to mine. "Oh. Okay. Ah, if you would just have a seat—"

"My brother and his wife, Clayton and Shelly Gable," Jackie snapped at her. "Where are they? I got a call that they were here."

The woman nodded before reaching for her phone. "One moment, please. I'll get someone to come help you right away."

"Lincoln Bates Rutherford Riscoff. How dare you come in here with her? She's not allowed to set foot in this place! I want her gone!" Lincoln's mother shrieked from a doorway near the entrance to the emergency area. His brother, Harrison, clung to her arm.

"Mother, please calm down. You're going to—"

Mrs. Riscoff's face crumpled and she burst into sobs, and Harrison pulled her against his side.

Lincoln looked at me, torn. "I'm sorry, I have to—"

"Go." My voice shook as I released his hand, hating that I immediately missed his strength.

Jackie slipped her arm around me.

"I'm sorry," he said again before he strode toward his family.

The triage woman finally made her phone call. I tried to look at her instead of watching Lincoln, but of course, I failed.

Lincoln's mother reached out and wrapped a hand around his arm, like she was securing him and making sure he wouldn't come back to me. She tugged on him as Harrison led her into a room beside the emergency sign, and the door closed behind them.

"If you could please come with me. There's a private room over here where—"

"Where are my parents? What happened to them?" I blurted out the questions because I couldn't wait another second without knowing *something*.

"It'll be a moment before the doctor can speak to you. Please come with me." She led us to a doorway opposite the room where Lincoln and his family went.

Jackie and I waited, huddled together on a teal vinyl couch for what felt like countless hours. Finally, someone opened the door. A man in a white coat appeared. A doctor, I assumed.

"Where are my parents? Why won't anyone tell me anything?" Whatever measure of calm I'd gained from Lincoln's presence had dissipated, and now I needed answers before I lost my shit and started screaming like Mrs. Riscoff.

"You're the Gable family? I'm Dr. Frances."

"Please tell us something," Jackie replied. "We're both going out of our minds."

He nodded solemnly. "Mr. and Mrs. Gable were involved in a car accident earlier this evening. We don't have all the details about the incident, but—"

Static ramped up in my ears. I could see it on his face. I knew what he was going to say.

"Oh my God." My voice broke on a sob. "No. No."

5

His expression turned grim. "We did everything we could, but we were unable to resuscitate either of them. I am so very sorry for your losses."

Pain and disbelief tore through me as tears blinded me. *They can't be gone. It's not possible.* My lungs seized, and I couldn't breathe.

"No. No. No."

Jackie's arms wrapped tighter around me as she rocked me from side to side.

"This can't be happening. This isn't real. They're not—"

"I'm so sorry, Whit." Jackie's voice cracked. "So sorry."

"I'll give you both some time, and when you're ready, if you would like, I can take you back to say your good-byes."

Good-byes? *No.*

Visions of their sheet-covered bodies invaded my brain, and I bolted for the trash can and dropped to my knees, dry heaving.

"I can't do this."

Jackie pulled my hair away from my face. "I'm so sorry, sweet girl. I'm so sorry."

I stayed on my knees, watching my tears drip onto the black plastic trash bag, and wondered if anything would ever be right in my world again.

Then I thought of my brother. "Oh my God. We have to tell Asa." My entire body trembled. "God, how do I tell him? What do I tell him?" My tears came harder and faster, and Jackie helped me to my feet.

As soon as I was upright, another realization slapped

me in the face. *I don't know what happened to Lincoln's father.*

"Oh my God. I didn't ask about Lincoln's dad. I have to know if he's—"

I rushed toward the door and tried to yank it open, but Jackie slammed it shut.

"You need to listen to me, Whitney. We've got our own mess of problems to deal with right now. You need to let the Riscoffs handle their own. I think it'd be best if you stay far away from that boy and his family. Nothing good can ever come of it."

# LINCOLN

I STARED down at the white sheet that covered my father.

*No, not my father. My father's body.*

My father was gone. He wasn't under that sheet.

I turned away to look at anything else. The wall. The silent machines. My mother's hunched form as she cried on my brother's shoulder. She'd pushed me away moments after I arrived and continued clinging to him.

Somehow, I couldn't stop myself from looking back at the sheet.

*How can my father be gone?* I'd seen him today. Hours ago. He'd been laughing with one of the interns, clapping him on the back for something the kid had done, and I'd been struck with a sharp stab of envy.

My father had never laughed and joked around with me when I was that age. I would have given anything to see that kind of approval on his face. Instead, I rarely saw his face at all. He was constantly traveling for business or working long hours.

He didn't teach me to play catch. My tutor did. He never saw me score a touchdown in boarding school because he could never fit my games into his schedule. He wasn't around to tell me about girls and sex and using condoms. My friends did, and then Commodore hammered it home when I was older. My father . . . was conspicuously absent from the memories of most of the important moments in my life.

I remembered the week before I'd found out I had to come back to Gable a couple of months ago. My father had flown out to New York City for a meeting, and we'd had dinner at one of my favorite places. He'd complimented my wine selection.

*And then immediately hit on the waitress.*

I pushed that memory away too, and stared at the sheet with silent regret until Commodore walked into the room. I didn't know where he'd been, but water dripped from his rain jacket.

He looked at the sheet. Then at me. My mother. My brother. He crossed the room and sank into the chair beside my father's covered body. I watched as he braced himself to lift the sheet. It was the first time I'd ever seen the old man's hand tremble like that.

As soon as he saw my father's face, Commodore's eyes snapped shut and he dropped the fabric.

"How did this happen?" His voice was rough and quiet but grew stronger and more demanding. "How the *hell* did this happen?" The question echoed in the room and down the hall.

His head snapped around, his gaze scouring me, my brother, and my mother.

"We don't know yet, sir," I replied.

My grandfather's jaw ticked. "I want answers *now*. My son is *dead*, and the Gables were involved. No one sleeps until someone tells me exactly how the hell this happened."

I cringed as he said *Gables*, but thankfully the doctor stepped inside the room.

"Mr. Riscoff? Sir, I'm so sorry I wasn't here when you arrived. I was with the man who arrived first on the scene. The police have finished interviewing him. If you'd like—"

"Get him in here!" Commodore's voice boomed.

The doctor nodded and backed out of the room.

Commodore's stare, harder than granite, landed on me. "I wasn't supposed to *outlive my son.*"

My mother looked up, her face contorted in anguish. "It should've been you. He said you called him back to the office. That's why he's dead!"

Commodore's brows swept together. "What the hell are you talking about?"

My mother's finger jutted out, shaking in the air as she pointed at Commodore. "He left tonight, in the middle of that storm, because you couldn't wait for some report until tomorrow. This is *your fault.*"

Commodore's face showed nothing but confusion, and that told me exactly what I needed to know. *My father wasn't working tonight. There was no report.*

He'd lied to my mother. Again.

Before Commodore could respond, the doctor returned with a man wearing damp clothing. "This is Mr. Ainsley, a volunteer firefighter. He—"

Commodore stood. "Let the man speak. I want to hear him tell us what happened. Not you."

The doctor's mouth snapped shut and he stepped back.

"I'm so sorry to you all for your loss." Mr. Ainsley removed his hat, and his gaze drifted to my mother. "Ma'am."

"Tell us something," my mother screeched, and I was afraid she was going to scare him out of the room.

Ainsley nodded. "I was heading home from picking up a buddy at the bar, and noticed the guardrail was out on the bridge. In that rain, I figured it'd be all too easy to lose control and for a car to go off."

"Which bridge?" I asked, because I'd driven over the bridge that was closest to Whitney's parents' house on my way from the cabin, and I didn't see anything.

"Downtown. Bridge Street."

I nodded, and he continued.

"I parked and got out and looked over the side, and I saw a woman on the bank. She wasn't moving. I called 911, grabbed my bag, and climbed down. That's when I saw the cars. Both of them were caught up on the rocks. One was upside down."

"Jesus Christ," Commodore whispered, bowing his head.

"I went to the woman because she was the only victim I saw at first."

"At first?"

Ainsley nodded. "I checked her pulse. Nothing. She wasn't breathing either. I tried CPR, but she was unresponsive. I stayed with her until the EMTs showed up. When fire and rescue came, we waded out into the river. That's when we found the others."

My stomach rolled as I pictured the scene he painted.

"My son would've been driving a Mercedes," Commodore said, his voice rough.

"Yes, sir. That's who I saw next. I'm sorry to say that . . ." He trailed off and looked at my mother. "You sure you all want to hear this?"

"Just tell us," Commodore said. "We need to know."

Ainsley glanced at my mother again, and his voice dropped low, almost like he was hoping she wouldn't hear. "Mr. Riscoff was underwater in the passenger seat when we found him."

My head jerked up and I stared at Commodore, certain the shock I was feeling was the same as what was reflected on his face.

"The passenger seat?" My mother's voice trembled, and suddenly I was terrified I was going to lose both my parents tonight—my father to an accident and my mother to a heart attack. "Who was driving the car then?"

Thankfully, she didn't grasp her arm or chest like she usually did when she was having an episode.

Her gaze darted around the room, from Ainsley to Commodore to me, and back to Ainsley again. "Who was driving the car?" she repeated, her tone turning shrill again.

Ainsley swallowed. "I don't know for sure, ma'am. The driver's seat was empty, and the window was open."

My mother shot to her feet.

"Mother, please, sit—" Harrison tried to calm her down, but she ignored him.

"He said he had to *work*. He was *working*." She said it to Commodore, as though hoping he could go back and make my father's lies the truth. I knew if my grandfather could, he would.

Commodore's face remained impassive. Nothing he could say would change what had happened. Nothing any of us said could.

My brother finally said what everyone in the room was thinking. "So she crawled out of the window . . . and left him in the car to . . ."

All the blood remaining in my mother's face drained away as she absorbed what Harrison had just said. "That Gable woman killed him! She murdered my husband! She—"

I crossed the room and crouched in front of her. "Mother, calm down. Please."

She spat in my face.

Shocked, I stumbled backward, blinking and wiping it away. *My mother just spat in my face.*

No one in the room moved or breathed as I rose.

"Don't you dare speak to me." My mother's voice turned sharp and deadly. "You walked in here tonight with her *daughter*! Sneaking around with that little Gable slut all summer was bad enough, but coming in the hospital with her tonight? You were probably in bed with that trash when her whore mother killed your father!"

# WHITNEY

AS I STOOD between the bodies of my parents, Mrs. Riscoff's words ricocheted off the walls of the ER like bullets designed to maim instead of kill.

*"You were probably in bed with that trash when her whore mother killed your father!"*

They shattered me, mostly because they were true. At least, if what the police officer just told us was true.

*My mother was having an affair with Lincoln's father.*

*My mother was driving Lincoln's father's car when the cars collided and they both went over the bridge.*

Aunt Jackie bolted for the door. "I'll kill that old hag myself if she says another word."

My body felt like it was shutting down, one system at a time. My brain couldn't handle everything that had been thrown at it tonight. My emotions were shredded, especially after the phone call I'd just had with my brother. Aunt Jackie had to tell him what happened because I couldn't force myself to say the words.

*I can't take any more.*

Numbness swept over me, and I embraced it.

"Whit? Baby? Asa said you were here. I was already almost to Gable when he called."

The voice was so familiar, but my brain felt like it was slogging through mud as I tried to identify it.

"What are you doing here? How did you—" Jackie sputtered as I looked up at the person standing in the doorway.

*Ricky.*

His gaze locked on the two sheet-covered bodies. "Fuck. *Fuck.*" Ricky covered his mouth like he was going to puke. "Shit, they're really—"

"What are you doing here?" I asked, sounding like a zombified version of myself.

He stepped toward me. "I got on a plane as soon as I got your letter. I had a shitty layover, otherwise I would've been here sooner." His gaze cut back to the bodies. "Asa just told me about . . . *Fuck.* I'm so sorry, Whit."

Ricky came to me and dropped to his knees at my feet. When he wrapped both arms around me and laid his head in my lap, I was too frozen to react. I didn't understand why he was here, but maybe that was because I didn't understand anything right now.

I let Ricky hold me as he apologized over and over.

"You need to keep walking, boy."

Aunt Jackie barked at someone, and my head jerked toward the doorway. Just before she pushed the door closed, my gaze collided with a tortured hazel one.

*Lincoln.*

A new storm of emotions rolled through me. I didn't know where one ended and the next began.

Pain. Regret. Loss.

What was broken tonight could never be repaired.

A Gable and a Riscoff could never be together. Fate would never let it happen.

# WHITNEY

*Present day*

"WHAT HAVE YOU DONE?"

The accusation in Lincoln's voice—the voice that just promised me a new beginning—shreds me.

"What are you talking about?"

He holds out his phone, shoving it toward my face. The damning headline is at the top in bold.

RICKY RANGO'S ESTATE CLAIMS HE WAS THE TRUE RISCOFF HEIR

I TEAR my gaze from the words and look back up at Lincoln. "You think—"

"I don't know what to think, Whitney. You were his wife. You have to tell me what the hell is going on."

I wish I could. I reread the headline before Lincoln lowers his phone. Any words I might try to speak get caught in my throat.

I look up at him, still attempting to form a response, but from the look on Lincoln's face, it doesn't matter. He's already tried and convicted me. *Again.*

Today, for a second, I thought I might not actually be cursed.

*Wrong.*

"Say something. Anything," he says as his phone vibrates again. He never looks away from my face, expecting me to have some kind of answer when I have *nothing* to give him.

I'm so tired of being found guilty of crimes I didn't commit.

Self-disgust, for letting this happen again, washes over me. *I'm the only one who can allow someone to make me feel this way, and I'm* done.

I straighten my shoulders. "I have nothing to say. Absolutely nothing."

He steps toward me, confusion creasing his brow. "Then—"

I hold up a hand to silence him as hysterical laughter bubbles up and spills from my lips. I don't care if I sound crazy. I don't care about anything but getting the hell out of here before he makes me feel any worse on a day that's already predisposed to be awful.

"You know what?" My voice cracks, and I clear my throat.

"What?"

"I already know how this little scene ends." I wave my hand between us. "So I'm gonna save you the trouble. You don't need to throw me out, because I'm gone."

I spin on my heel and head for the door. My shoes are nowhere to be found. *Again.* God, why is my life one big disaster repeating itself over and over?

I yank the massive glass door open just as Lincoln grabs my wrist.

"Whitney, wait—"

"Don't touch me." I shake him off and step outside. "I'm done doing anything you ask. You don't trust me? Then you don't fucking deserve anything from me."

I slam the door behind me. Three steps down the driveway, all the morally outraged stiffness fades from the set of my shoulders, and tears track down my face.

Every step of my bare feet on the asphalt reminds me that I never learn.

*But this time I will.*

I make the vow to myself as I walk away from Lincoln and out to whatever bullshit life throws at me next.

I just don't expect life to throw more bullshit at me so soon.

When I reach the final turn in the driveway, the dull roar starts.

*What in the ever-loving hell?*

Cameras flash above and through the black bars of Lincoln's gate, capturing my walk of shame.

*No. Not again.*

My stomach drops when the paparazzi gathered there recognize me.

*"Oh my God."*

*"That's her!"*

*"It's Whitney Rango!"*

How in God's name did the vultures find Lincoln so quickly? We're not in LA, and these aren't reporters from the *Gable Miner*.

The story he showed me must have broken early this morning or late last night for them to be here by now.

*"Whitney, are you and Lincoln Riscoff together?"*

*"Did you know that your husband was really a Riscoff?"*

*"Did you kill your husband so Lincoln could inherit?"*

*"How long has your affair with Lincoln Riscoff been going on?"*

With every question they hurl like daggers, I want to turn around and run in the other direction. But I can't. There's nowhere to go but back to Lincoln's front door, and my pride won't allow that.

*"Is it true that your dad killed Lincoln's father when he tried to run away with your mother?"*

The last question is like a punch to the gut. It shouldn't surprise me that they latched onto that nugget.

"No comment," I tell them as I take another step forward.

A rock digs into the ball of my foot, and I hop backward. It's like my body knows better than I do that I can't walk through that gate and face them. But what other choice do I have?

An Escalade slows as it turns off Gable Road and into the driveway blocked by the press.

*Great. Now they're bringing in the big guns.*

I stand frozen in the middle of the driveway, contemplating running into the woods. At least, until the Escalade's driver rolls down his window and orders them away.

The reporters at the gate don't listen. The Escalade moves forward, making it clear the driver has no problem running them over if they won't get out of his way.

That's when I realize it's not more press. Only someone with the name Riscoff would dare run someone over in broad daylight, in front of a crowd of cameras. It takes a lifetime to build up that level of arrogance.

The gate swings open, and shockingly, the reporters don't dart inside. They must be veterans, or at least well-versed in the consequences of trespassing.

The Escalade rolls to a stop beside me and the back window rolls down.

*Commodore.*

"I don't want to know why you're here, but get in."

I'm officially caught between a rock and a hard place. *Story of my life.* Who would I rather face? Lincoln or the patriarch of his family?

I remember that night when he helped me up out of the dirt at the cabin and drove me home. Commodore wasn't cruel like I'd expected him to be. I decide to take my chances with him.

It's the only way I can salvage my pride and escape the press.

I round the SUV and enter the back seat from the other side. Reporters shout questions at me, but I tune them out —a skill I've honed over the last decade but didn't know I'd need again so soon.

When I shut the door, it's blissfully quiet inside.

"Martin, take us home."

I jerk my head sideways to look at the old man. "I'm not going to your house."

He raises a snowy white eyebrow. "You're in my car. You go where I take you, Ms. Gable."

I open my mouth to argue, but he continues.

"Do you really think the press hasn't figured out where your aunt lives? No one will dare set foot on my property. I'd shoot them myself."

He has a point, even though I don't want to admit it. I offer up another solution.

"Drop me off at Magnus's. No one will bother me there or *he'll* shoot them."

Commodore studies me. "Fine."

As Martin drives through the gate, I keep my face pointed straight ahead, unwilling to look at them, even though they can't see me through the tinted windows.

"Would you care to tell me what the hell is going on?" Commodore asks. "Because we have quite the mess on our hands this morning, and it's all because of your late husband's estate."

"I saw the headline."

"And?"

I turn to look at the cagey old man. "At this point, I'm guessing you know more than I do. I'm not the executor of Ricky's estate."

He narrows his eyes. "Then who is?"

I'm somewhat surprised he doesn't already know. I thought Commodore Riscoff knew everything.

"Ricky's mom."

# LINCOLN

"*FUCK!*" I slap my hand against the back of the door Whitney walked out of, not knowing what the hell to think. She wouldn't defend herself, and to me, that implies guilt.

But I don't want to believe that. *I can't believe that.*

Then again, who the hell else could have done this? She was married to Ricky Rango. She has to be in charge of his estate. *Right?*

I head for the bedroom, throw on some clothes, and snag my keys from the counter in the kitchen.

Last time I sent her running, I was young and stupid, and I waited too long to go after her. This time, I'm not making the same mistake.

Five minutes from the time Whitney slammed the door, I'm in my Range Rover, hauling ass down my driveway . . . just in time to see my gate close behind a familiar black Escalade as it cuts through a throng of reporters.

Whitney is nowhere to be seen, but I can't miss the press camped out at my gate.

*Shit. Fuck. Goddammit.*

I call Commodore. *No answer.*

"Come on, old man."

I try his driver, but Martin doesn't answer either.

*Fucking hell.* I could strangle the meddling old man right now, but that's not an option. He already made it clear that he doesn't want me having anything to do with Whitney, and with this news breaking . . . he's likely to take her as far away from me as he can get. Or to someone who wants me with her even less.

Like her aunt Jackie. Whose house is probably already swarming with reporters too, if they've done any research at all.

My phone rings, and I glance at the display in my car. *McKinley.* My first thought is that something happened with my mother.

"Is she okay?"

"Who?" my sister asks.

"Mother."

"I haven't talked to her yet today. I'm at work. I wanted to know if you've laid the groundwork for me to get Jackie Gable back, or if you're still working on pulling your head out of your ass."

McKinley hasn't heard, which means she's a sitting duck.

"You need to double the security at the resort right now."

"What? Why?"

"Ricky Rango's estate filed a request for a paternity test to be performed to prove he was Dad's biological son."

My sister sucks in a sharp breath. "Are you serious? Is that why Whitney came back?"

"I don't know what the hell is going on, if you want to know the absolute truth. But I'm working on pulling my head out of my ass, so I need a favor from you and I don't want to pull rank."

"I'm listening." Her response is hesitant.

"I made a mistake this morning, and I need to fix it."

"Does this mistake have to do with Whitney Gable again?"

I don't know when my sister became so perceptive, but she is. "I need two suites on the VIP level of the resort to put her and her family in. The press is already swarming at my house, and I want to keep the Gables out of the line of fire."

McKinley's quiet for several moments before answering. "As long as Jackie Gable comes back to work for me, you can have whatever rooms you need. We only have a couple VIPs coming in this week, anyway."

"Thank you. I owe you, Mac."

"Don't call me that. And whatever you do, don't let Mother find out until you have a better explanation to give her than you did me. I'll tell the household staff to hide the newspapers, kill the cable and internet, misplace her cell phone, and tell her the cars are all in for repair, but that'll only work for so long."

A proud smile makes my lips twitch as she runs down the list of all the ways she's going to cut our mother off from the outside world. It's shockingly thorough. McKinley has learned well from Commodore on how to manipulate people.

"I like your plan. I'll work on finding out what the hell is going on."

"You do that. And, Lincoln?"

"Yes?"

"I would like for Mother not to have another episode if we can avoid it. None of us wants or needs that right now."

"Agreed. I'll do whatever I can to resolve this as quickly as possible."

"Is there . . . is there a chance that Ricky Rango could've really been our half brother?"

I answer with complete honesty. "I don't know yet. I'm trying not to jump to any more conclusions."

"Good. Because you can't see clearly when Whitney Gable's involved with anything. Pulling your head out of your ass should help."

The most unlikely of smiles tugs at the corner of my mouth again at my sister's advice. She grew up into a formidable woman when I wasn't paying attention.

"Duly noted." I hang up the call and roll toward the gate. It's time to run the gauntlet . . . and I'm not referring to the press.

I need to find Whitney, apologize, and get her to agree to stay at The Gables before the press destroys us all.

# WHITNEY

*The past*

MY BIG BROTHER'S strong arms rocked me from side to side. His hug was the first thing to shake me loose from the fog I'd been lost in for the last forty-eight hours.

Ricky had been here nearly twenty hours a day, and would probably never leave, but Aunt Jackie had kicked him out at night and insisted that I sleep. But it was impossible to sleep. Maybe that was why I felt like a walking zombie.

"I'm so sorry." I said it to Asa over and over, but I wasn't sure what I was apologizing for anymore—the loss of our parents, or being with Lincoln when it happened. Except . . . Asa didn't know about Lincoln and me since he'd only just walked in the door.

My brother released me and stared down at my face. "Do we have any idea what the hell Mom was doing with Riscoff?"

I looked away, not wanting to acknowledge the obvious, but Asa was no idiot.

"She couldn't have been screwing around with him," he said, answering his own question. "They've treated us like shit for years. She wouldn't."

Karma laughed from the kitchen doorway. "Didn't you hear, cuz? Gable women love the Riscoff dick. Just ask your sister who she's been sneaking around with."

I wanted to punch Karma in the face. She'd been hovering nonstop since Aunt Jackie brought me back to their house from the hospital, like she wanted a front-row seat to my grief. How could anyone be so cruel?

"Karma, get out of here. Give them some space," Aunt Jackie snapped, shooing her out of the room as Asa stared at me with disbelief.

"What is she talking about?"

I swallowed, not wanting to admit it, but I couldn't lie to my big brother. I'd never been able to lie to him.

"Lincoln Riscoff and I . . . we . . ."

Shock crossed Asa's face as he took a step back from me. "Fucking hell. This is my fault. I should've taken you with me and gotten you out of this town. You deserve better than this. What the fuck did I think was going to happen without anyone to watch out for you?" He shook his head, and I was stunned that he was blaming himself. "You're not staying here, Whit. We'll get through the funeral, then you're leaving with me."

Before I could respond, Ricky came up behind me, having entered the house through the front door so quietly I didn't hear him.

He threw an arm over my shoulder. "Not necessary,

man. She's coming with me. I fucked up, and I know it. I'm going to take care of her from now on. I promise."

I twisted out from under Ricky's arm, suffocated by the weight of their combined smothering. *Why can't anyone let me decide what I want? Why is everyone always trying to control me?*

I looked from my brother's face to his best friend's. They meant well, but it was too much. I just needed space so I could breathe.

"I can't talk about this right now." I took a step toward the kitchen, but Ricky caught my wrist and pulled me against his chest.

"I'll take care of you, Whit. No one will ever be able to hurt you again, especially not those fucking Riscoff assholes."

My brother watched us both. "Yeah, you fucked up, Ricky. And when you say no one will ever hurt her again, you better mean you too, jackass, or I'll take you out back and shoot you myself."

"I'm sorry, man. Shit got crazy for a little bit. It's the rock-star way. But Whit and I, we're a forever thing."

I tugged my wrist from his grip and stepped away before he could pull me back. "I'm not having this conversation. Not here. Not now. And not ever, if I have my way." Ricky and I hadn't talked about what he'd done, and I'd been too shattered to bring it up until now.

"Baby, I hurt you and I'm sorry. I know what I have with you is worth so much more. Please, just give me a second chance."

I felt like I was being pulled in too many different

directions, and it was going to tear my soul to shreds before I found my way.

"Just stop. Both of you. Let me have some peace!" My tears flowed again, and this time Aunt Jackie rescued me.

"You boys back off. Asa, I need your help finalizing funeral arrangements. We didn't want to make decisions without you here."

I didn't wait to hear any more. I ran upstairs to Cricket's room, where I'd been staying.

My phone showed a missed call. *Lincoln.*

I stared at his name. *What could he possibly have to say to me?*

Nothing I wanted to hear.

# WHITNEY

*Present day*

COMMODORE'S QUESTIONS become more pointed as Martin guides the Escalade up the mountain roads. I shouldn't be surprised that the old man waited until we're out in the middle of nowhere to really begin the inquisition.

"Did he ever say anything about his father?"

"Ricky never wanted to talk about his dad. Ever," I say with complete honesty.

"Did he say if his parents were married?"

I shake my head, wishing Commodore would quit with the questions. "He didn't talk about any of it."

"Where is his mother now?"

At least that's one question I can answer easily. "San Diego. She left Gable and moved down there after Ricky bought her a condo."

"But why wait so long to push for a paternity test?" The old man seems lost in thought, and I have no idea how to answer his question. His attention snaps to my face. "How old was Rango when he died?"

"Thirty-seven."

The old man's tanned face loses a few shades of color. "Which means he was born before Roosevelt married Sylvia." Commodore curses under his breath. "If my son married and divorced that woman without me knowing, her son could've been a legitimate Riscoff heir."

My stomach twists as he says the words. *Oh Jesus. This can't be—*

Commodore's heavy hand wraps around my arm, his fingers gripping tightly.

"What?" I jerk my chin toward him.

"Are you pregnant?"

My head flies back at the unexpected question. "No."

His gaze drills into me with enough intensity to frighten a hardened killer. "If you lie about this, I'll make your life a living hell. Do you understand me?"

I keep my voice as even as possible. "I'm not pregnant. I'll go pee on a stick right now and prove it if you really want." I yank my arm out of his grip. "But don't ever touch me again, old man."

He gives me a curt nod and looks out the window on his side of the Escalade.

The wheels in my brain spin out of control. Commodore's right. The only reason for Ricky's mother to try to have him legally declared a Riscoff after he died would be to get a cut of their fortune for a child. Ricky's child. Her grandchild.

*But that child doesn't exist. Does it?*

Ricky was cheating on me . . .

*This can't be happening.*

My mind races as question after question flies through my brain until one finally sticks.

*Why would Renee Rango wait until after Ricky died to file a paternity suit?*

The answer seems so blindly obvious, I'm shocked it didn't occur to me sooner. Ricky was her golden ticket to Easy Street—and now he's gone, and he left her nothing. She didn't even have enough money to battle the bank when it went after his future royalties. Royalties for songs I wrote.

That fact burns now more than ever before.

"All because of the money . . ." I whisper the words to myself, but Commodore's hearing is sharp, and his attention turns back to me.

"Why else would someone cause this big of a mess if they weren't after money? It always comes back to money."

"Not always," I say. "Some people don't give a shit about how much money your family has."

The old man's gaze narrows. "You may be the only person who could say that and I might actually believe you."

"Believe whatever you want, but if Lincoln's last name weren't Riscoff and he didn't come with a billion-dollar inheritance, things would've been a whole lot different ten years ago."

"I haven't settled my will quite yet, girl, so it's a good thing you're not attached to him for the money."

"I'm not attached to him at all," I say, my tone full of false confidence.

"I'd tell you you're lying, but you already know that."

I hate that Commodore calls me out so effectively, but even more, I hate that I'm this affected by Lincoln. I need to exorcise him from my soul. But if I couldn't do it over the last ten years, how in the hell am I going to do it now?

"You don't know shit, old man."

"Watch your mouth, girl. That temper of yours will be your downfall. If you let someone make you angry, you give them control over you."

"I don't need your advice on how to live my life. I'm doing just fine on my own."

He crosses his arms over his chest as the Escalade rumbles over a bridge, and one of his bushy white eyebrows disappears into his hairline. "You're a terrible liar, Ms. Gable." I turn away, but he keeps speaking. "You'd do well to learn that not everyone shares that quality. Be careful who you trust. Most people will never deserve it."

"So that's the Riscoff way? Don't trust anyone?" I say the words to taunt him, but Commodore nods.

"Proof before trust. Even with your own blood."

He goes quiet as we approach Magnus's driveway, but my brain is caught on what he just said. This is the man who groomed Lincoln to assume control of an empire from the day he was born. That sentiment has probably been drilled into him over and over.

I thought Lincoln didn't trust me because I'm a Gable. But maybe it's not personal. Lincoln probably doesn't trust anyone. *Even his own family.*

It's sad . . . but enlightening.

Martin shifts the SUV into park at the end of Magnus's driveway. Thankfully, there are no reporters waiting here.

I reach for the door handle and pause to look at Commodore. "Thank you for the ride."

"I would prefer not to have to rescue you a third time, Ms. Gable."

"I can see why. White knight isn't exactly your normal role, despite your hair and beard."

One corner of his mouth quirks up.

"Be careful, old man. You almost smiled."

"Good luck, Whitney Gable." Any lightness fades from his expression. "And what you told me—you tell no one else."

I give him a short nod as I climb out of the SUV and shut the door.

# LINCOLN

"Is CRICKET WITH YOU?" I ask Hunter, the next person on my list to call.

"Yeah, why?"

"I need your help getting her family to the resort with enough clothes to stay for a few days while things die down, and I need her to pack for Whitney."

My friend goes quiet. "While *what* things die down?"

"Ricky Rango's estate is claiming he was not only a Riscoff, but also would have been the rightful heir."

"Fuck," Hunter whispers. "His estate? Does that mean Whitney has something to do with it?"

"People keep asking me that, and I have no answer for you because she stormed out of my house after I asked her one simple question."

Hunter groans. "Please don't tell me she's trying to leave town again. You gotta quit fucking up with this girl, man. You're killing me here."

He's right, but it's not like I'm doing it on purpose.

When it comes to Whitney Gable, fucking everything up seems to be what I do best.

But that's going to change.

"I'm doing everything I can to stop that from happening, which is why I need you to bring all of her family to the resort and have Cricket pack Whitney's bags. I'm on my way to Jackie's to find her, and I'm guessing the press will be staking it out soon if they aren't already. They were outside my gate this morning, and I'm doing what I can to keep the Gables out of the line of fire. Putting them up somewhere I can protect them is the best solution I can offer while we figure this mess out."

"Is this going to fuck up my wedding and make Cricket unhappy?"

"Not if I can help it."

He groans. "That motherfucker Rango. I know I shouldn't ask, but do you think it's possible? Could your dad have—"

It's one question I haven't wanted to think about, but knowing my father . . . "Anything's possible at this point."

"And you have no idea if Whitney was in on all of this?"

I shake my head, but Hunter can't see it. "No."

"And you're going to protect her family anyway."

"Yes."

"Maybe you're finally getting your shit straight then." He pauses before continuing. "I'll talk to Cricket about her family. She'll stay with me until this goes away. I don't know how we're going to convince her mom to move into The Gables, though."

"Tell her about her promotion and raise. McKinley's ready to meet with her whenever she's ready."

"All right," Hunter says. "I'll see what I can do. I make no promises, though."

"One more thing . . ."

"Do I really want to hear it?" he asks with a healthy dose of skepticism underlying his tone.

"Your wedding at The Gables?"

"Yeah?"

"No charge. Not for a goddamned thing."

"You can't—"

"Don't argue. It's done."

As soon as I hang up with Hunter, I head for Jackie Gable's house. It's time to fix what I fucked up this morning.

## WHITNEY

I KNOCK and wait for the sound of the shotgun cocking. Magnus doesn't disappoint.

"Who's there? If you're trying to buy my land for that prick next door, you can walk your ass right back to his car."

"Uncle Magnus? It's Whitney."

The floorboards creak as he shifts to look through the window. "You playing Benedict Arnold now?"

"He gave me a ride. I . . . I got caught without one this morning."

"Walk of shame? Thought you were old enough to know better, girl."

I release a long breath and try to ignore the embarrassment that goes with it. "Can I please come in? Or do you want me to walk my Benedict Arnold-Scarlett Letter ass back down the driveway where the press might see me and descend on you too?"

He opens the door. "What press? What the hell is going on now?"

"Can I come in?"

Magnus eyes me up and down like he's afraid I'm carrying Riscoff cooties. Which, of course, I am. I mentally add a shower to my list of things I need so I'll feel less like an idiot.

He glances over my shoulder as if looking for the reporters I mentioned. "Get yourself inside."

I come in and head straight for his percolator to help myself to some coffee. Magnus watches as I take the first sip and release a sigh of relief. Coffee is life, and I'm hoping it's going to miraculously turn this day into less of a shit show. It's a long shot, but I'm willing to try.

"You gonna tell me what kind of situation we got now that involves those news vultures?"

I take a few more sips of coffee before I tell him what little I know about the news article Lincoln shoved at me on his phone. Being mindful of Commodore's warning, I stick to the basics, including the fact that I'm not the executor of Ricky's estate.

"Sounds like someone got a little greedy and wants a piece of the Riscoff pie. Can't say I blame them." He holds out his coffee mug for a refresh, and I oblige. As he sips, he eyes me. "So, whatcha gonna do?"

"I don't know yet."

"The timing seems awful coincidental. I don't remember much about your mother-in-law. She the type to try to make you look bad?"

Renee Rango is the last person I want to think about

right now, because all I want to do is run her over with Commodore's Escalade for creating this shit storm.

"You could say that she and I never really bonded." It's the politest understatement I can make.

"Single mom with an only child?"

I nod.

"She probably wouldn't have liked anyone he picked."

I laugh. "Ricky was her little prince. He could do no wrong. But none of that matters now. I need to talk to her because she has a hell of a lot to answer for."

"You think you could trust her word? Don't know that I would."

He has a good point, and it reminds me of what Commodore said about trust. Namely, that I do it too easily.

Magnus keeps talking. "If I were that asshole Riscoff, I'd make her pony up evidence before I'd give her the time of day."

I don't want to wait for Renee to dig up evidence. I just want it all to go away.

"I can't help but wonder if she's doing this for more than just the money."

"What do you mean?" Magnus asks.

"Maybe she'd back off if I slipped out of town and disappeared."

He leans back and crosses his legs at the ankles. "You gonna keep letting other people decide how your life goes? Or are you going to figure out what it is that you want?"

Again, the old man's question reminds me eerily of the man he claims to hate. Maybe they're both right. Maybe

I've been letting people push me around for so long that I don't know how to stop.

Magnus apparently thinks I'm taking too long to answer his question. "It sounds to me like all you want to do is keep running from your problems and hoping they won't follow you. Let me be the bearer of bad news, kid— that ain't gonna work."

"Bringing my problems back to Gable didn't exactly work either," I reply in an attempt to defend myself.

"Your problems started in Gable. It's the running that didn't work. You ever think about staying in one place and facing them, and see how that goes down?"

I clasp the mug in my hands and bring it closer to my body, trying to absorb some of the heat. "Won't staying just make it worse? The press won't leave."

He shrugs. "You won't know until you try. It seems like you've made the same mistake a few times. Why not make a different one and see how it feels?" Magnus leans forward, resting his elbow on the counter. "When you get to be my age, you realize life is a whole lot of bullshit peppered with a few important things. But until you're my age, you're gonna mistake a whole lot of that bullshit for the important things. You need to figure out what you want out of this life, kid. Find the people you want to share it with and hold them close. *That's* one of the few things that actually matters."

I soak in the wisdom I didn't expect to hear this morning and turn it around in my head, looking for flaws. I can't find any.

"How'd you get to be so smart?"

"I'm almost ninety years old, and I live out here alone

because I learned all that the hard way. Don't do what I did. Don't hang on to something that doesn't matter so hard that you can't let it go to reach out and grab what does."

Is that what I'm doing? Holding on to the past so hard that I can't grasp what's happening in the here and now?

What happened a decade ago between Lincoln and me colors every moment of our present. We talked about a fresh start, and then everything went to hell moments later when we actually needed to communicate with each other about something important.

With the benefit of some distance and a little fortifying coffee, I think about this morning's situation.

*Did we both just overreact?*

Lincoln's words were most definitely an accusation . . . but from the way that article was written, how could he come to any other conclusion? Any outsider looking in would assume I was the one in charge of Ricky's estate.

*And Lincoln has been taught not to trust anyone.*

"And the last piece of advice I got for you—if you think life is going to hand you nothing but shit to eat, that's all you're ever going to see on your plate. You gotta look for the good to recognize it, kid, or you'll miss it completely." Magnus points out the window and up at the sky. "I could see that blue sky, or I could focus on the one cloud hanging there. When you get to be my age, you don't have time to let a few drops of rain ruin your entire day. It might be your last."

He has a point. In my parents' house, everyone was always looking for the bad. Probably so much that we missed out on a lot of the good. It's a habit I've never truly broken.

Magnus whacks his mug down on the counter. "We got company." He grabs the shotgun and makes it to the front door quicker than someone his age should be able to move.

"What are you—"

When he swings the door open and fires a few rounds into the air, I scream, spilling my coffee all over the floor. With my ears ringing, I stare at him like he's lost his damned mind.

"What the hell is wrong with you, Magnus?"

He holds out the shotgun to me, barrel pointed up. "You want to take some potshots at the feller coming up the driveway? Bet you haven't tried that yet."

I peek out the window. Sure enough, Lincoln's walking up the gravel drive with both hands over his head.

# WHITNEY

*The past*

THE WHOLE WORLD passed me by while I retreated into my fog where nothing felt real. Some days, I felt like I'd stepped outside my body and was watching life as a play while other people acted it out.

*How can my parents be gone?*

I was starting to wonder if it would ever feel real. Part of me hoped not. That might be more than I could handle.

I heard Asa on the phone with the bank. Dad hadn't paid the mortgage since they bought the house, and they were going to foreclose. The only way we could stop it was if we paid off the entire loan. They wouldn't even listen to reason about letting us catch up on the payments.

Asa's temper snapped as soon as he hung up the phone. "It's because Commodore motherfucking Riscoff is on the board. They won't cut us any fucking slack." He said it to

Aunt Jackie, but I was pretty sure the whole neighborhood heard him.

*So now I'm going to be homeless.*

Our parents didn't have life insurance or a single dime of savings. Mom and Dad were supposed to be buried in their plot at the cemetery, but Asa only had enough saved up from his army pay to cover a cremation. Aunt Jackie offered to take out a second mortgage to buy caskets, but Asa wouldn't let her.

His reasoning? "What do they care now, anyway? They're dead. We can bury their ashes instead. There's no point in making you go into debt to buy a box where they can rot."

Even though his crude words had made me cry, he'd had a point. It still hurt to know that the choice was taken from us because of money. But right now, everything came down to money. Mostly the fact that we had none.

I was a coward for letting Asa and Jackie deal with everything, but what help could I really offer in this situation? *None.*

So instead, I stared at the light green wall of Cricket's bedroom from where I was curled up on her bed. I crushed her pillow to my chest and wished I could live anyone else's life but my own.

I'd almost managed to doze off, but the front door of the house slammed and Asa yelled.

"Get the hell off our property, motherfucker! You aren't welcome here."

My chin jerked up as my entire body started to vibrate. There was only one person who would piss Asa off that badly solely by existing.

I rolled over on Cricket's bed, and it was the fastest I'd moved in days. I ran to look out the window, and sure enough, Lincoln stood in the driveway.

Asa stalked toward him, using the rifle in his hand to point at Lincoln's truck, and his voice was loud enough to filter through the single-paned glass.

"You get back in your truck and get the hell out of here, Riscoff."

"I need to talk to her."

"Well, I'm the one with a gun. So, *fuck no,* you aren't seeing my sister."

"I—"

"Rango already told me all the bullshit you spouted off at him. Whatever you think you had with Whitney? It's just as dead as our folks and your dad."

I winced, hating how cruel Asa was being. Lord, if he knew I'd run down the cabin's gravel drive barefoot after Lincoln threw me out, he'd shoot Lincoln dead right where he stood.

The tragedy that followed might have relegated our fight that night to the level of *doesn't matter at all in the grand scheme of things*, but I wasn't sure I'd ever forget the sting of the sharp side of Lincoln's tongue.

*He made me feel like trash, and I never want to feel like that again.*

If there was any thought in my head about leaving the house to battle with Asa in order to hear what Lincoln had to say, that thought stopped me.

"You can't keep me from seeing her. Not forever," Lincoln said, and Asa let out a harsh laugh.

"Maybe not forever, but for long enough that it won't matter anymore."

I didn't know what my brother meant by that, because his leave wasn't going to last much longer.

Lincoln stood his ground until Asa raised the gun and sighted in on his head.

*Oh Jesus. No.* My heart seized and I grabbed the latch of the window, prepared to throw it open and scream down the neighborhood.

*I can't bear to lose him too.* I didn't know where the thought came from, but Lincoln took a few steps back toward his truck.

"That's right, Riscoff, you keep on fucking walking. And remember, I know a hundred ways to kill you that don't need a gun. You ever try to talk to my sister again, and that's exactly what I'm going to do."

"You can try," Lincoln said. "My family would bury you."

Asa stepped toward him again. "Come back here, and I'll bury you first."

Lincoln climbed into his truck and drove away. I sank to the floor, tears I didn't remember crying tracking down my face.

# LINCOLN

*Present day*

"YOU LOOKING TO DIE TODAY, SON?" Magnus Gable calls from the door of his house, shotgun in hand.

*What the hell is it with Gables and meeting people with guns?* I've braved one before to talk to Whitney, and I'll do it again and again.

"No, sir. I'm here to talk to Whitney. I was on my way to her aunt's house when Commodore told me I'd find her here instead."

"Don't know that she wants to talk to you, boy. She might shoot you, though."

"That's a chance I'm willing to take, but before she does, I need to tell her I'm sorry for this morning. I'd really like to apologize face-to-face."

Commodore told me everything he'd learned about Ricky Rango and his mom from Whitney, but I didn't need to hear the details to know, beyond a shadow of a doubt, that she wouldn't have come back to try to snake a piece of the Riscoff fortune. She could have had it before, but she made it clear that she wanted nothing to do with me or it.

In fact, Whitney's the only woman I've ever met who wanted me *despite* my last name and our money. But I fucked that up in the end too.

When I called Commodore, he warned me to leave her alone. I don't give a shit what the old man says or threatens. I'm not letting him manipulate this situation anymore. I'm going to fix what I broke this morning, and pray Whitney will give me a real fresh start, even if I don't deserve it.

Last night is burned in my mind, and so is the softness in her eyes this morning before I blew it all to pieces.

"Might want to say that a little louder, son. Not sure she can hear you."

At any other time, this might be embarrassing, but I put aside my pride. "Whitney, I'm sorry."

"For what?" she yells. "Being an asshole?"

I take a few more steps forward, even though I'm making myself an easier target. "For not waiting to hear what you had to say before I jumped to conclusions."

"You mean never trusting me?"

I look up at the sky. She had to go straight for the kill.

She's right. I have trust issues, especially when it comes to women. My father and Commodore instilled them in me from the time I was a kid. They made it clear that every woman would want something from me because of my last name.

*But Whitney was never like that.*

"Yes. I should've trusted you."

"Why should I believe you now?"

"Oh, that's a good question, girl. I like it," Magnus crows from the doorway where he acts as the peanut gallery while blocking Whitney from my view.

I wish I was doing this without an audience, but when you fuck up like I did, clearly you don't get that luxury. "Because I wouldn't put myself out like this for anyone else."

"I don't think that's a good enough explanation," the old man says.

"Please, Blue. You don't have to believe me yet, but I'm going to prove it to you. I want to protect you and your family from whatever comes out of this mess. I've got rooms for all of you at The Gables. The press won't be able to get to you there. You'll be safe and have your privacy back."

I hear a *humph* from Magnus before he steps to the side and Whitney's dark head peeks out of the doorway.

"My entire family?"

"I ain't goin'. I can take care of myself," Magnus says, gesturing to the sky with the shotgun.

"Everyone you can talk into coming. I already have Hunter and Cricket working on your aunt and your cousin."

Whitney's expression is skeptical, and that's fair. I can work with skepticism—as long as there are no bullets flying in my direction.

She glances at Magnus. "Can you give us a few minutes?"

He eyes me shrewdly. "You try anything shady and I'll pepper your ass with buckshot, boy."

"I understand, sir."

Magnus backs up, and Whitney comes out of the house to meet me in the driveway. It kills me when I see she's still barefoot.

"I've got your shoes in the car. I'm so fucking sorry, Blue."

"Screw the shoes, Lincoln. What's the catch?"

"What catch?"

"Riscoffs never do anything without an angle or a motive or strings attached. So, what is it this time?" The woman who trusted me this morning has been replaced with a more cautious and cynical one.

"I deserve that. No angle, except for keeping you away from the press, which is why you left LA to begin with, right?"

She crosses her arms over her chest. "I'm not going to sleep with you."

I jerk my head back. "Is that what you think of me?"

Her face stays expressionless. "I'm working on not thinking about you at all. I've let people hurt me too many times, including you. For years, I thought that's all I deserved. But you know what? I was wrong. I deserve a hell of a lot better, and I'm not settling for anything less ever again. Based on this morning, and how quick you were to see me as the enemy, I don't know why I'd give you another chance to get close enough to hurt me ever again."

Buckshot would have been less painful than Whitney's swift and efficient delivery of the truth.

She's right about everything.

I may have aged ten years, but my knee-jerk reaction

this morning shows that I haven't learned a damn thing. I don't want to be another guy on the list of people who hurt her. I want to be the man to protect her from the world.

"I know I fucked up, Blue. I don't deserve another chance. I'm not even going to ask for one this time. Right now, all I want is to give you a safe place to go while I try to figure this out."

She watches me, her somber expression creasing in confusion. "Why even bother then?"

"Because I have something to prove—to you and to myself," I say, and I've never meant anything more.

## WHITNEY

I DON'T KNOW what Lincoln's game is, but I straighten my shoulders and meet his gaze dead on. It's been a long time since I've had the courage to stand up for myself, and making that speech, telling him how much he hurt me, gives me confidence I didn't know I could have.

He may have something to prove, but so do I.

I'm done being the girl who lets the rest of the world dictate her future. It's time to figure out what matters to me and own it.

Lincoln's offer is probably the best possible solution for avoiding the media shit storm Ricky's mom unleashed, but I don't trust him not to change his mind.

"How do I know you'll keep your word and won't turn us all out the second you decide I'm somehow to blame for this?" I pause, deducing how he must have known I was here. "Or did Commodore tell you everything already?"

Lincoln's gaze narrows. "I knew the second you walked out my door that I made a big fucking mistake. I'm trying to fix it. Please, let me protect you the best way I know how."

Dealing with the paparazzi in LA was the worst part of my life for the last ten years. And then when they turned feral after Ricky's death? It was straight out of a nightmare.

While I'm not going to trust Lincoln blindly, the smartest thing I can do right now is take the protection he offers and keep him at a distance. I don't want to subject Jackie and Cricket or Karma and her kids to the aggression I've endured with the media, and this may be the only way to avoid it.

I lift my chin. "Fine, but I'm only doing this for my family."

He nods. "I understand. Thank you for letting me help."

———

IF YOU WOULD HAVE TOLD me two hours ago that I'd be driving through the front gates of The Gables with Lincoln Riscoff to stay for an extended period of time, I would have asked where the crack you were smoking came from. But here I am, and Jackie, Karma, and the twins will be here shortly too.

The last two times I was here, things didn't exactly work out well. Maybe there's some truth to the saying that the third time's a charm? I'm keeping a healthy dose of skepticism close regardless.

A bellhop comes running when Lincoln pulls his Range Rover under the massive covered entrance to the hotel.

"Mr. Riscoff, welcome. We've been expecting you, sir. We have suites prepared for your guests." He hands Lincoln a white-and-gold envelope. "Here are your keys."

"Thank you. Make sure you have the day manager show Jackie Gable and her daughter to their suite when they arrive."

"Yes, sir. I've already been briefed. We'll do everything in our power to make sure they have an excellent stay and all their needs are met."

Lincoln thanks him and then helps me out of the car.

Part of me is grateful for the lengths Lincoln is going to in order to make sure my family is shielded, but I can't shake the feeling that everyone is watching us as we walk through the lobby of the hotel.

*Quit looking for the bad, Whitney. Let's be positive for a single day.*

I can do this. I'm not the same girl who felt completely out of place here ten years ago. I've had dinner at the White House. Met the queen of England. Flown in private jets. I may never have felt like I belonged at Ricky Rango's side, but I sure learned how to fake it. And that's exactly what I'm going to do now.

"Looks like you've done a lot with the place." I inject humor into my tone as I scan the decor, because it's clear the gilded interior hasn't changed, although it doesn't look like it's aged either.

Lincoln's lips quirk with a smile as we step into the elevator. "You know how Riscoffs are. We don't handle change well."

I look sideways at him, intending to make some kind

of snarky comment, but instead I see him wave a card across the reader and push an unmarked button.

"Do I need to be worried that you're taking me to the dungeon?"

He raises an eyebrow. "Really?"

The elevator starts to rise, and I shrug. "Well, we're not going down, so I guess that answers my question."

"We're going to the top floor of this tower. It's reserved for VIPs . . . celebrities, foreign dignitaries, politicians."

"We don't need that." Apprehension coils in my chest. "We don't want special treatment."

Lincoln studies my face for several moments before he replies. "You deserve it, and you're getting it. I'm not going to argue about it."

I don't give a shit that he doesn't want to argue about it. I open my mouth to object, but he keeps going.

"Any employee or guest can access the other floors, but not this one. Access is very limited because we host people who require the utmost privacy, and McKinley is absolutely rigid with security. It's the one place where I'm confident the press can't get to you, which makes it the best place for you."

I think of Jackie facing screaming reporters like I did. Oh Lord, if they got their microphones in Karma's face . . .

The thought of what my cousin would say if given the chance is the deciding factor.

"Fine, but only because I don't want my family to deal with the things I've had to."

Lincoln's mouth, already open no doubt to deliver another reason why I should agree, snaps shut.

I like seeing surprise on his face instead of feeling it on mine. Maybe keeping him off-balance should be my new goal, because it's the best shot I have at a level playing field.

*Why would I want a level playing field if I'm not giving him another chance?*

"I'm sorry you had to deal with any of it." Lincoln sounds sincere, and something that looks like protectiveness flickers to life in his hazel eyes. "If it's within my power, I'll make sure you never have to again."

I want to believe him, but I remind myself that I'm no longer taking Lincoln at his word. *I'm going to trust as little as he does.* It may not be what Magnus meant when he said try something new, but it's the only strategy I have right now.

My decision quells my rising tendrils of anxiety, and I paste a polite smile on my face. "I guess we'll see."

I pull my shoulders back just in time for the doors to slide open, and it takes everything I have not to gape.

If I thought the lobby, restaurant, and spa at The Gables were opulent, I hadn't seen anything yet. This floor puts even the nicest hotels I've ever set foot in to shame. Even the fresh, crisp scent of the air is more exclusive than what I was used to in my old life.

I step out onto white marble floors shot with gold and silver, waxed to a shine so high that I can see my own reflection.

"The lounge area is to the right. There's a fully stocked bar with a bartender available twenty-four hours a day."

He waves to the gleaming white, gold, and silver slab of marble that curves around the side of the huge space filled with white leather seating arrangements and marble tables. The windows beyond the bar almost overshadow the space, however, because the view from up here is absolutely incredible.

I wander toward the wall of windows. One section slides apart as we approach, revealing the shimmering blue waters of a pool and white padded lounge chairs. Not a single person is outside, despite the gorgeous sunny day.

"No one uses this?"

Lincoln pauses. "Rarely. We only have two guests on the floor right now."

My gaze trails along the intricate molding, taking in the details. "I don't even want to know what this costs for a night, do I?"

"Does it matter?"

It may not matter to Lincoln, but I don't like the beholden feeling I'm already letting creep in. *No. I will not feel guilty about this.*

"I guess not," I say, trying to keep my tone blasé.

"Let me show you to your room. Unless you want a drink first?" He inclines his head toward the bartender.

The last thing I need right now is alcohol to muddy my decision-making abilities when Lincoln is being so accommodating.

"The room, please."

I try to ignore his smile when he waves his hand toward the hallway. "If you'd follow me this way, I'll show you to your suite, Ms. Gable."

Maybe the room isn't a safe choice either.

*No, Whitney. Stop. You're not going to be the one who goes back on your word immediately.*

59

I follow him down to the last door on the right side of the hallway. Lincoln pulls the envelope the bellhop gave him from his suit pocket and waves it in front of the card reader, then opens the door.

Of course, I expected something opulent, and the living room of the suite doesn't disappoint. It's all white and gold and absolutely gorgeous. My gaze catches on the massive fireplace with a gold mantel along one wall and the cozy chaise near it. I can already picture myself curled up there with a journal.

"Will this work for you?" Lincoln asks.

I turn around, immediately thinking he must be making a joke about it, but his expression is completely serious. *He really cares if this is okay.*

"It's perfect," I reply honestly. I'm about to say something else when I hear excited little-girl squeals echoing down the hall.

*The family has arrived.*

"Oh my gosh, Mommy! Did you see?"

Lincoln and I step out of the room to see Jackie herding my cousin's kids behind a man leading them to another room down the hall. Karma trails after them, her attention on her phone and not on her kids.

"Girls, please. Quiet. There are other people." Of course, it's my Aunt Jackie hushing them because Karma can't be bothered.

I hurry toward them. "I'm so sorry, Jackie. I didn't know—"

Karma looks up from her phone, her resting bitch face on point. "You didn't know what? That reporters would be camped out on Mom's front lawn trying to get my kids to talk to them?" Her tone is cutting. "Nice, Whit. Real nice."

"Karma, not now," Jackie says.

My cousin jerks her head to the right and glares at my aunt. "Then when, Mom? Because I had to pull my kids out of school because of her."

"It's not Whitney's fault. I'm afraid that if there's blame to be laid anywhere, it's squarely on my family."

Heat radiates off Lincoln's body as he steps up behind me. It takes a few moments for my brain to recognize that *he's standing up for me.*

But Karma can't be so easily placated. "There's a lot of things we could blame your family for today."

"Karma!" My aunt snaps out her name, but Karma's face is still screwed up with anger.

"Then again, if Whitney doesn't care that her parents are dead, why should we?"

Grief slices at me, which is certainly her goal. *She just had to bring that up.*

Another voice joins the fray before I can reply.

"I think we all have reasons to be sad today. I'm sorry our family histories are connected with tragedy." McKinley Riscoff's soft tone is filled with strength and carries the slightest hint of rebuke aimed at Karma.

"I need a nap. I'm tired." Karma grabs each of her daughters by the hand and disappears inside the suite.

We all stand in awkward silence for a moment before Lincoln's hand brushes mine as he steps beside me and looks from me to my aunt.

"I think we can agree that we all wish many things involving both our families would've happened differently.

61

And most recently, we need to apologize for our mother's behavior. She was out of line." He glances at McKinley.

"I have a written apology from her to you, Ms. Gable." McKinley pulls a small envelope out of her suit jacket pocket.

Aunt Jackie's eyebrows shoot up, and I'm sure my face mirrors hers. "Did you hold her at gunpoint?"

McKinley's laugh cuts through the tension in the air. I swear, I can almost feel Lincoln relax a few degrees beside me.

*No. I shouldn't be so in tune with his reactions. I don't care about him anymore.* Although I remind myself of the facts, my brain and body seem to have stopped communicating.

Jackie opens the note and scans the contents. "Well, those are words I never expected to read."

"I hope you'll accept my offer to return. We would really like to have you come back and work here."

Jackie stiffens, and she's quiet for a moment. "I would like to say no. More than anything." She pauses and swallows. "But that's my pride speaking, and surely it cost your mother even more of hers to write this note."

"You could say that," McKinley replies.

"Then I think I can be the bigger person and accept your offer. I've never had a problem with you, Ms. Riscoff, and I truly enjoyed working here."

"Then we would be pleased to have you rejoin us as assistant day manager."

Jackie's expression betrays only the smallest hint of her excitement. "If your mother's not going to have another heart attack because of it, I would like that."

"Wonderful." McKinley Riscoff's smile is genuine. "If you'd like to come down to my office later today, we can go over the details, and you can meet with your new immediate supervisor."

"Thank you, Ms. Riscoff," Jackie says with a nod. "I appreciate the opportunity."

"You earned it."

"I should be going too." Lincoln steps toward his sister, and I curse the fact that my body immediately registers the new distance between us. "If you need anything at all, please don't hesitate to press the majordomo call button on your phone. Each suite has been assigned someone, and you'll be in good hands."

"And feel free to call for room service, use the spa, pool, fitness center, or anything else we have to offer," McKinley adds. "We want to make sure you're truly comfortable."

I meet Lincoln's gaze and choose the simplest response possible. "Thank you."

# WHITNEY

I FOLLOW Aunt Jackie into the suite she's sharing with Karma and the girls. A quick glance around the space tells me it has three bedrooms and must take up a quarter of the floor.

"Is this really going to be okay with you?" I ask her.

Jackie spins around to look at me. "Are you serious, Whit? Do you have any idea where we are? The rooms on this floor are some of the most expensive in the whole country. I might have to swallow some pride, but when the options are this or dodging reporters on my front lawn, I'm not about to say no to living in luxury for a while."

"I'm so sorry about that—"

She holds up a hand. "Don't start apologizing for more stuff you didn't do."

The fact that my aunt doesn't even question what's going on reminds me that she's been on my side for my whole life in a way no one else has ever been.

Before tears can start burning my eyes, I change the

subject. "And the job? Are you sure you're okay with that too?"

"More money, better hours, and more authority? I think I can handle it just fine."

I look at the closed door that Karma must be behind. "And what about Karma?"

Jackie's lips press together into a flat line. "I don't know what it is this time with her, but I'm going to figure it out. I swear, that girl just doesn't know how to be happy. I don't know where I went wrong with her, but I'm damn sure trying to do better with my grandbabies."

The closed door flies open, and I don't even know why I'm surprised. Karma is the queen of shitty timing.

"If you're going to talk about me, at least make sure I can't hear you."

"Were you listening at the door?" I ask her. "Because I thought you were napping."

"The bed's uncomfortable."

I stare up at the ceiling, needing some kind of divine patience and finding none. "Seriously, Karma, for one freaking second, can you stop being so damn negative about everything?"

Her glare intensifies. "Why should I? To make you feel better about the fact that all our lives revolve around you and always have? Am I supposed to be happy you finally get something for spreading your legs for Lincoln Riscoff?"

"Karma!" Aunt Jackie snaps out her name.

I take a long look at my cousin. Her blousy shirt is wrinkled and dark circles line her eyes.

"I'm sorry for whatever I did to you. I'm sorry that

I've interrupted your life. I'm sorry that because of me you're forced to stay in the nicest place you've ever seen."

"You're not sorry for anything, Whitney. But you will be someday." She shuts the door in our faces and disappears inside.

"I don't know what I did to make her hate me so much." I release a long sigh.

Jackie's expression turns rueful. "I think you got the life she wanted—out of this town, with a man who wrote you love songs. She's bitter because she feels like she never got what she deserved."

"Too bad she's got it all backward," I say with a shake of my head.

Karma and Jackie have no idea that I wrote all those love songs myself, wishing someone would actually feel that way about me. But they don't need to know.

*The past*

"Baby, please. I know it'll help. I swear. You've been keeping everything bottled up, and that's not healthy. You won't even talk to me."

There were a lot of reasons I hadn't talked to Ricky, and while the biggest one was that I was drowning in my own grief, I was also still fucking pissed at him.

*But if he hadn't cheated, I wouldn't have met Lincoln.*

Immediately, I wanted to slap myself for the thought.

*Stop, Whitney. That doesn't matter. It's over. It never should have happened to begin with.*

"Come on, Whit." Ricky held a pencil near my hand and pushed a spiral notebook toward me. "Just start writing down words like you used to when we'd drive around. It doesn't have to make sense now. You'll fix it later."

When he wrapped my fingers around the pencil, I

squeezed it so tightly I thought the wood would snap, but it didn't.

Because it wasn't a pencil. It was a pen.

That's how out of it I was. I couldn't see anything clearly through my haze.

"Baby, I'm worried about you. You just need to let it all pour out of you. Music is the best way to do it. You know that's what I did when I thought I lost you."

*When I thought I lost you?*

Like it was past tense. Like he already had me back.

*Does he?* No one had consulted me in that decision— or had I been too out of it to realize that had happened too?

*Lincoln hasn't come back . . .*

Another thing that didn't matter. *Because Riscoffs and Gables can never be together.*

All I wanted was to stop thinking about all of it. I wanted to stay in my haze, but it was fading before I was ready to deal with the real world again.

My fingers gripped the pen, and I stared down at the lined paper.

Maybe I could find some oblivion if I could get it all out. Maybe then these emotions haunting me would live on paper in a song and not in my head. Then I could go back to feeling *nothing*.

My hand started to move as if of its own accord.


*Regret. Pain. Shredded soul.*

Ricky read the words out loud from beside me. "That's a good girl. Get it out. It'll heal you."

My hand kept moving, and I wrote through the tears that started to fall.

*I hate you for doing this to me. I hate even more that I can't hate you anymore.*

"That's fucking gold, babe," Ricky whispered, and I hunched forward, not wanting to hear his voice.

"Go away. Leave me alone."

He moved back. "But—"

"I want to be alone, Ricky."

He stood and raised both hands. "Okay. But write it out. You know you'll feel better."

I listened for his footsteps and the sound of the closing door before I flipped to a new page.

In huge letters, I scrawled something at the top of the page.

*Long live regret.*

# LINCOLN

*Present day*

I DRIVE TOWARD MY OFFICE, and it takes everything I have to leave the resort grounds knowing that Whitney is there. McKinley and I discussed security, and she doubled it and is bringing in extra help just in case. Thankfully, the gates around Riscoff Holdings keep them away from me while I'm at work.

Unfortunately, those gates can't keep my brother out.

When I walk into my office—which should have been locked—he's standing near the window, enjoying the view while he drinks coffee.

"What the hell are you doing in my office?"

Harrison spins around with a smug smile on his face. "I wondered if you'd ever show up."

"Get the hell out."

"I don't think so, brother. As a vice president of this company, I'm entitled to a briefing on what the fuck is

70

going on. I heard you put your whore and her whole family up at The Gables after she brought another media shit storm down on the family."

My entire body tenses, and I take another step into my office, ready to crush his face with my fist. "Don't you fucking call her that."

"Doesn't matter what I call her—she's the one responsible for this mess."

It takes everything I have to rein in my temper. "You don't know jack shit about what's going on, so go back to your office and get to work on the projects assigned to you."

He walks toward me. "So you can run this company into the ground, thinking with your dick like you always do when it comes to her? I don't think so."

"Get out before I throw you out." I force out the words from between clenched teeth.

Harrison laughs. "Go for it. I'll make sure Commodore knows."

"He'd probably give me a raise. Now, get the fuck out of my office. I'm not going to ask you again."

My brother glares but heads for the door.

I take a seat at my desk, wishing that I could have a normal relationship with my brother and he wasn't raised hating me because he was born second. His bitterness over losing out on any piece of a billion-dollar inheritance will never fade, and that means I can never let my guard down around him.

He stops at the threshold and turns. "Oh, I forgot to tell you. We didn't make the auction deadline for the company you wanted. Missed filing the bid by three minutes."

*That motherfucker.* I stand and stride across the room. "You can fuck with me all you want, but when you start fucking with this company, that's where I draw the line."

He shrugs, and there's nothing I want more than to put my fist through his face. "Maybe if you'd been working last night instead of out chasing a piece of ass, it wouldn't have happened. I guess we'll never know."

"You were in charge of this bid. It was your responsibility. Twisting the truth won't work."

"I had a question for the boss . . . and you weren't around to answer it."

It doesn't matter what I say or do, Harrison will never take responsibility for his own mistake. I wouldn't put it past him to have missed the deadline on purpose. In fact, that's probably exactly what he did.

"Get out of here before I make the call to have you fired."

"I'd like to see you try." Harrison smirks before he leaves, shutting my door behind him.

*Goddammit.* I stalk back to my desk and narrowly resist putting a hole in the wall. The last thing I needed was another fucking problem to deal with today, but my brother always comes through at the least opportune time.

I pick up the phone and make a call to someone who might be able to fix what Harrison has fucked up. I should call Commodore, but that will wait until I have a solution.

Harrison may be a tattletale, but I'm a fucking CEO who gets things done.

EIGHT HOURS LATER, the sun has set, but I've finally arranged to have our late bid accepted for the auction. It took unanimous approval of the other bidders, which I wouldn't have been able to get if I hadn't called in an old favor from a man who scares the fuck out of them all. *Jericho Forge, I owe you now.* The move won't win me any friends, but that's not what I'm here for.

I pick up the phone to call Commodore, but he doesn't answer, which seems to be the pattern of the day. I don't know what the old man's game is this time, but I'm not playing it.

I've already lost ten years of the life I wanted, and I'm not going to risk losing Whitney again. I fucked up badly enough this morning, and I have a long road to fixing things with her and regaining her trust.

When she looked at me from Magnus's doorway, I saw the change on her face before she spoke the words. It gutted me to hear how I've hurt her, but I deserved that and more.

I'm older, wiser, and I know better—and yet I'm still making the same mistakes. But not anymore.

I push away from the desk and stand to stretch. I told Whitney I had no ulterior motive and that I only wanted to protect her and her family. That's true.

But there's another unspoken truth that goes along with it—I won't not let this opportunity pass without giving everything I have to do what I failed to do once before.

*Make her fall in love with me.*

I'm not a man who accepts defeat, even in the face of impossible odds. If there's a single chance that I can win Whitney Gable, I won't back down.

# LINCOLN

*The past*

I WASN'T TOO proud to admit that I had people watching Jackie Gable's house. I'd been waiting for another chance to try to talk to Whitney, and as soon as I got the text that Asa Gable was gone, I jumped in my truck and hauled ass over there.

When I knocked, footsteps came and I tensed, readying myself to see her face.

Except it wasn't her.

No, it was Ricky Rango.

*Fucking hell.*

My guy must not have known Rango was here. Then again, how would he? Mr. Rock Star didn't have a fucking car to signal that he was here.

"What the fuck do you want?" Rango stepped out of the house and shut the door behind him before crossing his arms over his chest. He was going for the tough-guy act, but the tattoos wrapping around his arms didn't intimidate me.

"I'm here for Whitney."

"She's busy."

"She'll get unbusy to see me." I didn't care that I sounded arrogant. This asshole needed to know that I wasn't impressed by him or his fifteen minutes of fame.

"If it's up to me, she'll never see you again, Riscoff."

*This fucking prick.*

"Good thing it's not up to you."

"It damn well is. She's my girl. Always has been and always will be. Doesn't matter if we hit a few bumps in the road. Whitney and I are for life."

I controlled my temper because all I wanted to do was sink my fist into this asshole's face. "You fucked around on her, she dumped your ass and then fell for me . . . and you're calling it a bump in the road?"

His nostrils flared.

*Good, now we're equally pissed off.*

"She didn't fucking fall for you. She's been in love with me since she was a kid."

I forced a smile onto my face. "I hate to break it to you, asshole, but she's not a kid anymore, and she's too smart to ever give you another chance."

A car pulled into the driveway behind me and the doors slammed. I whipped around to see Asa Gable. *Fucking great.*

"I told you to stay the fuck away from here." Whitney's brother came toward me, his face stamped with the urge to kill.

"Asa, don't you dare touch him," Jackie said as she walked toward us.

"Why? Because his family would make sure I'm shipped off somewhere and killed by friendly fire?"

I took a step down the driveway. "I don't know who the fuck fed you all these lies about my family, but we don't give two shits about you, Gable."

"Both of you, stop." Whitney's aunt waved an arm between us, then looked at me. "You should go."

"I need to see her. Please. Just let me talk to her for two fucking minutes."

Something that looked a lot like sympathy flashed across Jackie's face, but she shook her head. "I don't think that's a good idea right now. She's . . . not coping well."

The anguish leeching into Jackie's expression and the rough edge of her voice sent a slash of pain through my insides with enough intensity to double me over. I stayed standing because there was no way I was going to take a hit to my pride in front of these people.

I met Jackie Gable's gaze. "Can you at least tell her I've been here twice?"

Her expression softened, but Rango jumped back into the conversation.

"Twice? What the fuck?" He bolted toward me, his fists clenched.

I kept my attention on Jackie. She was my only potential ally here and knew how Whitney felt about me before. *Hopefully still feels about me.* And she was the only person here who would give me a single fucking chance to see Whitney.

"Please tell her I was here, and that I'm sorry. I'm so fucking sorry."

Jackie squeezed her eyes shut, and she was a moment away from giving in. I could feel it. But Asa responded for her instead.

"My sister has a double funeral to worry about, Riscoff. She's not gonna give a single shit what you have to say, now or ever."

I spun toward him, anger filling my gut. *They think they're the only ones who've lost someone?*

"I've got a fucking funeral to attend too, and I'd care if she came to my house and had a single word to say to me."

"But she hasn't come to your house, and she won't." Rango's voice might as well have been gasoline tossed on the fire of my rage. "Because she doesn't want a damn thing from you. She's got her family and me, and she doesn't need you."

I moved toward him, ready to fight, not caring how it would end.

"Please, Lincoln. If you care about her . . . just go." Jackie's tone, begging and defeated, stopped me cold.

*Not now. Not like this.* I raised my hands in front of me like I was giving up, but that's one thing I'd never do when it came to Whitney.

"I'll go, but I'll keep coming back until I finally get to see her. Talk to her. Apologize to her. I owe her that much."

From the expressions on their faces—rage and sadness —I knew they'd never let it happen.

That just meant I'd have to find another way.

## WHITNEY

THEY THOUGHT I couldn't hear them, but the yelling outside was impossible to drown out, even with my humming.

I sneaked to the windows in the living room but stayed pressed against the wall beside the panes. I couldn't let Lincoln see me, because I knew if I went outside, they'd tear me apart like jackals.

I couldn't handle seeing him with an audience. What we'd had wasn't for public consumption, even if he thought it should be.

We were better off as a secret. Something that was just *ours* and no one else's.

As I listened to them argue, I realized how naive he and I had been, thinking that anyone would accept us. Maybe in a world where no one knew our names, but here in Gable? We'd been cursed from the start.

I finally heard a car door slam, and my heart was so

torn as to what to think or feel in that moment, I barely reacted in time to run back to the kitchen before they stomped into the house.

"Why the fuck didn't you tell me he was here before?" Ricky barked the question at Asa.

"Because I handled it. She's my sister, asshole. I don't need to explain myself to you."

"She's my girl."

"Which means I'll fucking kill you—in more painful ways than I'd kill him—if you ever think about cheating on her again. Do you fucking hear me?"

"It was a mistake, man. I swear. I got caught up in all the LA bullshit. It showed me what really mattered. She's the only girl who wants me for *me* and not because of my song on the radio, and I didn't realize what I had until I fucked it up. I'm going to do everything to make it right. I swear I'll never hurt her again."

"You've been my best friend for twenty fucking years, Ricky. I don't make idle threats, so don't make me kill you. Now, go fucking try to get her to stop crying so damn much."

I sat back down at the kitchen table and wrote until my hand cramped.

*We were destined to go down in flames
Because every sin begets a sin.
Maybe someday I'll forget your name,
But until then . . . I never want to see you again.*

THE WORDS SPILLED out of me, but I knew I was lying to myself. I'd never be able to move on without seeing Lincoln at least one more time.

# WHITNEY

*Present day*

LIGHT STREAMS in through the window, and I open my eyes to see the most incredible sunrise over the gorge. Nothing, not even remembering the reason I'm here, can detract from the beauty of this moment.

*Because I'm looking for the good.*

Maybe Magnus was right. Maybe I've been focusing on the clouds instead of the beauty of everything else.

But this morning, even after a night filled with dreams of Lincoln, things look brighter and more vivid. Even the clouds are stunning, washed in orange, pink, and red. It's one of those moments that you can't help but be glad you're alive to see.

I wait for the sky to change colors before I pick up the phone on my nightstand. My majordomo answers immediately.

"Good morning, Ms. Gable. Can we bring you a latte or coffee before breakfast?"

"Coffee would be great."

He goes on to ask me what I'd like for breakfast, and I decide to indulge with a strawberry crepe. He returns with the coffee within minutes.

It's a different kind of luxury than I'm used to. At least, it feels different. Before, I was always part of the Ricky Rango entourage, where his needs came first and everyone else was an afterthought, especially me. I wasn't part of the band, and no one was ever allowed to know what my true role was. Ricky went out of his way to give the impression that I was just along for the ride and contributed nothing.

For some reason, that always made me feel like I had to prove that I was earning my keep. I went above and beyond, busting my ass to make sure every part of his life went smoothly, so people knew I was pulling my weight.

As his popularity grew, things spiraled out of control. Ricky pushed me harder, always wanting more. Different. Bigger. Better. It was never enough. If a single didn't hit number one, it was always my fault.

*And I let him make me feel like that.*

*I let him walk all over me.*

*I let him bully me into keeping his secret.*

Until the moment I found out he had gone back on his one promise to me and cheated.

Just like everyone else, Ricky Rango didn't realize what he'd had until he lost it. I finally grew a backbone *—and then he killed himself.*

For months, I've struggled with the guilt.

*Did standing up for myself really make him push that needle into his vein? Did he know what he was doing when he shot that fatal dose? Could I have stopped it?*

I can't put these questions out of my head. Maybe it makes me weak, but I think it makes me human.

*I'm not responsible for Ricky's actions.*

The thought materializes in my head and I grasp it like a drowning woman being thrown a life ring. It grows stronger with every breath I take, and the more I allow myself to believe it . . . the more liberated I feel.

I stare out at the gorge and focus on the blue sky between the clouds.

*I won't let his actions drown me in guilt for the rest of my life.*

*I won't let him steal my future because I'm stuck in the past.*

I take a deep breath and soak in the beautiful view. I've never meditated before, and I have no idea if that's what I'm doing, but as I let go of the negativity, I feel lighter than I have in months. A few moments later, words start coming to life in my brain, and my fingers itch for a pencil and paper.

It's not a song. I don't know if I have any of those left in me, but it's a voice that won't go silent until I get the words out of me and onto paper.

I rush to the desk and find a stationery set with a beautiful pen in a decorative inkwell. As soon as my fingers wrap around it, I second-guess myself.

My songwriting ability was equally a blessing and a curse.

But maybe . . . just maybe . . . getting the words out is

a way of letting go of the past. Maybe this is exactly what I need to do to give myself any kind of shot at having happiness in my future.

*I can write anything and it doesn't matter. No one will ever see it or read it. It can be just for me. An outlet.*

Giving myself permission is like flipping a switch. As soon as the pen touches the paper, I lose myself in the words and time ceases to matter.

Line after line, I unburden my brain from the guilt and negativity that have been dragging me down.

A pattern takes shape, and I flip to a new page. The lines start to rhyme. A chorus chants in my brain. Absently, I hum a melody, and my body rolls with the beat.

It should scare me. I should throw down my pen and back away from the desk, but instead of fear, I'm filled with an undeniable sense of power.

What I'm writing has meaning.

It's my truth.

I put words on paper until my hand cramps and my brain finally goes quiet, and the only sound in the room is my calm, steady breathing.

I stare down at the scattered sheets and realize that for the first time in a long time, writing words that will become lyrics fills me with purpose. Maybe because it's out of instinct and not duty?

With my hand wrapped around my now cold mug of coffee, I rise and walk to the windows. I don't know what time it is, but it doesn't matter because all I see above me is sunshine and blue sky. The clouds don't even register.

A smile tugs at my lips. *So this is what it's like to feel optimistic about the future.*

I finish my cold coffee just as someone knocks on the door.

*Probably Jackie taking a break.*

I turn and walk to the door, my step a little lighter. I don't bother to check the peephole before I pull the door open with a smile.

But it's not Jackie. It's Lincoln, and he's holding a takeout bag.

"Edward called me, worried that you hadn't ordered lunch or left the room. I told him he didn't need to report your every move to me . . . but I thought maybe you'd like to eat."

I blink, staring at the bag as he raises it higher.

"Cocko Taco."

"Did Cricket tell you it was my favorite?"

Lincoln shakes his head. "No. You told me once."

"And you remembered?" A strange feeling pangs in my chest.

"I remember everything, Blue."

We stand there for the longest moment, staring at each other in the doorway.

I bite down on my lip, because it's on the tip of my tongue to say *I do too.*

## LINCOLN

"CAN I COME IN?" I ask.

Whitney continues to stare at me, shock evident in her expression. I probably deserve to have her slam the door in my face, but thankfully she doesn't.

"Only because you brought tacos."

She turns and walks toward the marble slab table, leaving me standing in the doorway. I don't waste time following behind her.

"If that's what it takes . . ."

She glances over her shoulder at me with a raised brow. "Don't push your luck, city boy."

Her use of the nickname she gave me the night we met gives me hope that I haven't completely fucked this up for good.

"Besides, they're really my *second* favorite tacos, so don't go letting your ego get out of control."

I set the bag on the table and decide that this challenging version of Whitney is a hell of a lot more intriguing than the girl who let me have my way.

When I pull the tacos out of the bag—enough for about a dozen people because I hedged my bets by pretty much ordering the entire menu—she starts laughing.

"Seriously?"

"I wanted to make sure I got what you liked. Whatever we have left over, we can give to the staff. No one says no to tacos."

Her gaze cuts up toward mine. "Thoughtful of you."

But I don't want to talk about employees or how they're like family. In fact, I want to stay as far away from any topic that's likely to have us tiptoeing around to avoid land mines.

"If Cocko Taco is second best, where are your favorites from?"

Whitney chooses two foil-wrapped tacos and a few napkins. "Torchy's in Austin, Texas. You have to order the Trailer Park, served trashy. It's life-changing."

"Trashy?" I ask as I make my selections.

"With queso. If you don't order it that way, you're literally missing out on life. Fried chicken with queso is *everything*. And their guac." She moans. "Seriously incredible."

To anyone else, it might feel like inconsequential small talk, but to me, this conversation is the best I've had all day. I latch onto the information she gives me like it's a golden nugget.

"Sounds like you've been there a few times."

She nods and takes a bite. "Some days it feels like I've been everywhere . . . but also nowhere at the same time."

I follow her lead and unwrap my taco. "What do you mean by that?"

She tilts her head to the side as if she's trying to figure out how to explain it. "Before I left here, I wanted to go everywhere. It took a while before I realized that not all travel is created equal. When you're hitting a new city every day, all you see is hotel rooms and venues and backstage. It all looks pretty much the same. So, while I've *been* to hundreds of cities, I haven't *experienced* hardly any of them. No tourists sites. No landmarks."

I nod. "I know what you mean. I've been to big cities all over the world—and seen their finest conference rooms."

"Seeing the Eiffel Tower from a hotel window isn't exactly the same as standing under it at night, staring at the lights."

I chew the bite of my taco, and I'm in complete agreement with her. I've seen a lot of things . . . while on the way to and from meetings. But rarely have I had a chance to experience the culture of the places I traveled because there just wasn't time.

"So, where would you go first if you were to choose for yourself?" I ask, opening the guac and pushing it across the table toward her.

Whitney snags a chip and scoops up a glob before crunching down on it and letting out a small moan. After she swallows, she reaches for a napkin.

"Back to Austin first for tacos, obviously," she says with a laugh.

"Seriously?"

"Maybe as a pit stop on my way to the Indian Ocean.

I've seen it from a plane window, but I want to stand in that crystal-clear water of the Seychelles."

Part of me wants to know where the hell she was flying to see the Seychelles, but that's not important. What's important is making the visual in my mind—Whitney standing in the water up to her knees, wearing a tiny blue bikini—a reality.

"Seychelles sounds incredible," I reply, reaching for another taco. "So, how did you manage to discover Torchy's Tacos if you didn't get to see more than the hotels and venues?"

"There was a veteran roadie from Austin on all the tours. He was actually an amazing bass guitarist, but he wouldn't ever audition for a band because he never believed he was good enough. Every time we rolled into Austin, his sister would show up within an hour and she'd have all his favorites. He asked me to join him one day, and I was hooked. After that, he always saved me some because he knew how much I loved it."

It shouldn't surprise me that Whitney would make friends with roadies or that they would make sure she always got her favorite tacos. Whitney's sweet. Smart. Witty. Sarcastic.

Sitting around and eating lunch with her is the best part of my day.

This is what drew me to her before—how easy it was to be around her. How often she made me laugh and smile. It wasn't just the insanely addictive chemistry, although I can't not think about that too.

Whitney Gable is, by definition, the whole package. Unfortunately for me, she's also the one who got away. It hammers home exactly how stupid I was back then. I knew what I had, and I lost her.

*And then I had her yesterday morning . . . and fucked up again.*

She was totally right when she told me she deserved better. She does. She deserves the best I can give her, and I'm going to bring it. No more fuckups. No more mistakes. No more regrets.

*One step at a time,* I remind myself. I have to take things slowly and earn her trust back. Maybe that was our problem last time. We had one speed, and it was full tilt.

What I want from her isn't a sprint to the finish—I want the marathon.

I purposely keep things light, and we trade stories as we finish eating our lunch. When I cross the room to toss the empty wrappers in the trash can beneath the desk, scattered pieces of hotel stationery spread out on top of it catch my eye.

They're covered in her handwriting.

I know I shouldn't be prying, but I'm hungry for every bit of information I can get about Whitney.

It looks like . . . poetry? Then I remember what Ricky Rango had claimed—she wrote him a love letter.

"Are you a writer?" I ask as I glance over my shoulder at Whitney.

She bolts out of her chair and rushes across the room.

"Oh, God. Don't look at those. They're . . . nothing. Really, nothing." She practically hip checks me out of the way to get to the desk and shuffles the papers together. "I just write stuff. Sometimes."

"Is that poetry?"

She jerks her head up with a nervous laugh. "Oh, hell no. I'm no poet. I wouldn't even call myself a songwriter, really. No matter how long I've been doing it."

"A songwriter?" I ask as she clutches the papers to her chest. "You wrote songs? Like . . . for Ricky Rango?"

Whitney takes a step away from the desk. "Does it matter?"

"I'm just curious. I remember . . . I remember he said you wrote him a letter."

She looks away. "I didn't write him a letter. He sent me a shitty love song, and I fixed it out of habit and sent it back. That's what I did for Ricky for years. Fixed his shit. And then he just gave up writing completely . . . and it was all on me."

*She didn't write him a letter. She fixed his goddamn song. She wrote his goddamned songs.*

"That lying piece of shit." I say it more to myself than her, but Whitney huffs out a breath.

"Oh, you have no idea. He might have been a crappy songwriter, but Ricky was a great liar. All the way up until the end. Even his last freaking social media post that set all his fans on me like rabid dogs. He neglected to mention that the reason I filed for divorce was because he gave me an STD from some woman he was cheating on me with."

My brows hike up. "He cheated on you?"

She looks up at me, her lips pressed together. "Yeah, apparently he never stopped, and I was too stupid to realize it. But when I found out, I was done. I might have been a doormat for most of my life, but I never will be again. Oh, and for the record, I'm clean. I took care of that immediately."

"I wasn't worried about that, but I am glad you took a stand. You're right—you deserve a hell of a lot better."

"It took me a while to realize that." She looks out the window, and her voice quiets. "My brother would have killed Ricky if he hadn't . . ."

Asa isn't the only one who would be lining up to bury Rango for what he did to Whitney. And now . . . now he's haunting both of us.

"I'm so sorry, Blue. I wish I could go back and change everything."

She turns back toward me, and instead of looking broken, she straightens her shoulders. "It happened. It's over. Now I have to live with the consequences and figure out what's next."

More than anything, I want to be first in line for *what's next* with Whitney Gable, but that's not what she needs from me right now. I can offer her a safe haven to start rebuilding her life, and in the process, do everything in my power to earn the right to be a part of it.

But there's one thing that doesn't quite make sense.

"You wrote or cowrote Ricky Rango's songs for his whole career?"

She nods. "I sure did. His first number-one hit, "Summer Thunder"? I cowrote that when I was nineteen. Then there was his first platinum album, *Long Live Regret*. He didn't write a single song on it."

"How did I not know this?"

"No one does. I'm not listed as a songwriter or cowriter on any of them. Ricky convinced me that he would look bad if he wasn't the one writing all of his own music. He was terrified people would think he was a poser."

*That piece of shit.*

I keep my rage locked down because wanting to kill a dead man isn't going to help anything. But still, something here doesn't add up. According to Hunter's information from Cricket, Whitney is broke. According to Whitney, Rango's mom is the executor of his estate.

I'm still trying to figure out how to ask the questions in my head, when Whitney says, "And now his mother is the sole beneficiary of the mess he left behind. It wasn't much, because the bank took everything. She couldn't even afford to fight the bank for the future royalties because she didn't save a penny of the fortune Ricky spent on her over the years."

My rage blooms into something even sharper. "You've got to be joking. You wrote the songs. He took credit for them. And he left you *nothing*?"

Whitney nods slowly. "I spent ten years of my life busting my ass on his career, making him look like the rock star he claimed to be . . . and I walked away with nothing. But at least I got to walk away."

My brain is spinning with how to fix this for her. How she could get back her hard work. "I'd have to talk to my legal team, but you should be able to file a copyright suit against the estate and the creditors. Prove that you were the writer and didn't consent to the assignment of the future royalties."

"Sure, if I had a mountain of money I was sitting on." She slaps the papers down on the desk. "But that's not the case, and right now, all I want to do is move on."

The thought of her walking away from a decade of number-one songs and platinum albums kills me.

"But you can't let this go. I'll fund it."

Whitney whips around to face me. "No way in hell. First, I'm not a charity case. I wasn't before, and I'm not now either. Second, how do you think the press and Ricky's fans would react if I destroyed his legacy by telling them the truth—that he didn't write any of the shit they thought he did? I've already been through hell with them. I'm not doing it again."

I press my fingers to my temples. "I want to help. We can figure this out."

"I'm not asking for your help. I'm telling you that some things just aren't worth the cost you have to pay to get there. It's not worth it right now."

"So you're just going to walk away without a fight? Give up a decade of your life with nothing to show for it?"

Her plan is absolutely insane to me. It would be like me turning my back on the last ten years at Riscoff Holdings.

Whitney straightens. "Yes. That's exactly what I'm going to do."

"You can't."

THAT MAN DID *NOT* JUST TELL me I couldn't do something.

Oh, wait . . . yes, he did.

Because Lincoln Riscoff is the heir to an empire and thinks he knows everything about everything.

But he doesn't. He hasn't lived my life. He doesn't know what kind of hell would rain down if I made the claims he's suggesting.

That confidence I felt building earlier took a small hit when I admitted that Ricky had been cheating on me the entire time we were together, but it comes back as Lincoln challenges me. Mostly because this conversation sparks an idea that hasn't occurred to me until just now.

I cross my arms over my chest and smile. "Actually, Lincoln, I can do whatever I want, and you don't get a say."

He opens his mouth, but I'm not done. I nod at the stack of papers on the desk.

"If I want to do it again, I could. I thought there were

no more words left in me. No more songs. But I think I actually just wrote one . . . and that means there are plenty more. I don't need to take Ricky's legacy from him. I can make my own."

It's the most empowering thing I've ever thought in my entire life.

*I have a skill. A talent. Something of value to offer the world that no one else can replicate.*

My songwriting turned a kid from Gable into an international rock legend. That's . . . that's amazing.

*How am I just now realizing this?* I lift my gaze to Lincoln's, and I can't read his expression.

"Are you sure that's what you really want? Because there's no shame in building on the foundation that someone else laid."

Now I know exactly what he's thinking about—Riscoff Holdings. Probably because that's been the focus of most of his life.

"I'm not saying there's anything wrong with it. This isn't about you and your family, Lincoln. This is about my life and my choices. For the first time in maybe *ever*, I don't give a damn what anyone else thinks is right for me. I'm making my own decisions, and I won't let you change my mind."

He shoves his hands in his pockets, and I wonder how much it's costing him not to take over. Part of me expects him to try to bulldoze me, and I wonder if in my newfound confidence that I have enough backbone to stand up for myself. I brace myself, ready to try.

"You're right. I'm sorry. Whatever you want to do, I'll help any way I can."

I blink twice, thinking I must have imagined the words that came out of his mouth, but he continues.

"I'll always think it's bullshit that he took advantage of you, though."

Something warm wells up in my chest, and the sense of power I felt gains force.

"I let him take advantage of me," I reply, owning the decision I made. "But not anymore. I'm done letting people take advantage of me."

Lincoln studies me, and even though his hazel gaze is intense, it doesn't make me uncomfortable. "I can respect that."

For the first time in our entire history, I feel like the balance has shifted so we're on equal ground.

# LINCOLN

IT TAKES EVERYTHING I have to stop myself from acting on instinct—to push Whitney to pursue the copyrights and get what she's entitled to.

Rango used her for a decade and fucked her over in so many ways that if he weren't already dead, I would destroy him.

But it's not my choice. It's Whitney's choice.

And when I said I can respect it, I meant it.

Now, as much as I want to drag out our lunch for the rest of the day, I know it's not a good idea. *One step at a time.*

I gather the leftovers of our taco feast and head for the door, but I can't stop myself from pausing before it. "Would you like to have dinner with me tonight? I can bring more tacos."

Her cheeks flush, and my fingers curl around the doorknob to keep from crossing the room to pull her against me and end this afternoon the way I really want to.

"I was planning a family dinner tonight to celebrate my aunt's new job, so I'm technically busy."

"Rain check?"

Whitney's teeth close over her bottom lip, and there's nothing I want to do more than tug it free with my own.

"I don't know if that's a good idea. Maybe . . . maybe we should leave the past in the past."

The note of uncertainty in her tone gives me hope. I release the handle and step toward her.

"Is that what you really want, Blue?"

The shake of her head is infinitesimal, but it's all I need. I drop the bag of tacos on the floor and close the distance between us.

I stop six inches away, my heart kicking against my chest, because what happens in the next sixty seconds can change the course of the future I've always wanted.

"We both know I don't deserve another chance to hurt you, just like you said. If you give me one more opportunity, I vow on my father's grave that I won't make the same mistakes I did before. I can be the man you need me to be."

Her lashes lift, and her blue gaze is still uncertain. "Magnus told me I need to make different mistakes this time around. I don't know if this is what he meant, though."

She reaches out with both hands and clutches my shoulders, pulling me toward her until my lips crush against hers. I let her take what she needs from me, meeting her halfway, but don't steal control of the kiss. Blood roars in my head before diving straight to my crotch.

*No woman has ever affected me like Whitney Gable. Not before. Not since.*

Through it all, I keep my hands at my sides, because a single movement from me would end with us both naked on every flat surface in this room.

She finally pulls away. "You can take me to dinner later this week, but only if Cricket and her fiancé can come too."

I force my expression to stay neutral instead of grinning. Maybe other men would be annoyed, but I'm not. I'll take small victories whenever I can get them.

Whitney not wanting to be alone with me? That's all the proof I need to know that she's no more ready to leave us in the past than I am.

"I'll talk to Hunter."

Whitney inclines her head with a regal nod, and I return to the door, pick up the bag I dropped, and let myself out.

# WHITNEY

As soon as the door closes, I take two steps toward the sofa and plop on the luxurious cushions. My head drops back, and I stare at the ornate coffered ceiling.

*I kissed him.*

I kissed him and held on to my pride and my dignity and the upper hand.

A smile tugs at my mouth.

*I even gave him an order.*

That knocks free a little giggle and a burst of pride.

Trying to manage a man like Lincoln is like sneaking up on a mountain lion out in the woods, tweaking his tail, and jumping back, hoping you don't get mauled.

Totally stupid. Definitely crazy. But completely exhilarating.

My better judgment has already rendered its opinion—stay far, far away. But the rest of me can't abide by that decision.

My head flops sideways, and my attention catches on the stack of hotel stationery on the desk.

I still can't believe I told him I wrote Ricky's songs. Telling someone not related to me by blood felt *good*. The fact that Lincoln now knows that whatever Ricky told him before he threw me out of the cabin ten years ago was bullshit feels even better.

And seeing the rage on his face when he realized how badly Ricky had screwed me over? That was gratifying too.

I've never had someone in my life who was willing to go to war for me, other than my brother, and even then, he picked the battles. He didn't let me have a say.

Lincoln actually reined himself in because I told him to. I wasn't lying when I said I wasn't interested in trying to challenge Ricky's legacy. It would be a bloodbath, and it's not worth the cost right now.

The last thing I need is more death threats like the ones I got in LA. And with the press already in Gable and targeting my family? Not a chance in hell.

I spend another hour wandering the rooms of the suite, stopping with every rotation to jot down lines on my last blank sheet of paper. When I run out of space, I replace the pen in the holder and stare at the phone.

On a whim, I punch the button for the spa. Within two minutes, I have an appointment to see Gabi in the next hour.

---

"You came back," Gabi says as she wraps me in a hug. "I

heard you were staying here, but I wasn't sure if you'd come see me again."

"I promised I would."

She releases me with a crooked grin. "You should know, I heard that Lincoln Riscoff not only brought tacos to the front desk break room a little while ago, but word on the street is that he was joking and laughing. Pretty much everyone was speculating on his good mood."

"Oh Lord. I'm sure the rumor mill is hard at work."

"Honey, it's been working overtime since you walked into town. Follow me, and I'll catch you right up while I work on you."

As she leads me to the treatment room, I tell her, "To be honest, I kind of thought if I made an appointment, we could just catch up. I really don't need another facial. It's only been a couple days."

"*Psh.*" Gabi waves a hand. "Don't say that. I've been excited about this since I came out of my last appointment."

"But I didn't come down here to make you work. I wanted to get out of my room and see a friendly face."

She pauses at the doorway. "Here's the deal—I'll feel guilty getting paid if I don't do it, and I prefer to talk and work at the same time."

I step inside the room, inhaling the lavender-scented air. "Only if you're sure."

"Positive. I'll have your skin glowing by the time we're done."

As soon as I'm settled under the blanket, she starts to talk.

"The first thing I gotta tell you is that Maren Higgins is on the books today with an appointment."

I tense. "Oh, really?"

"Mm-hmm. I'm guessing she heard Lincoln put your whole family up—on top of Ms. Riscoff promoting your aunt—and rushed to get the first open appointment so she'd have a chance to get a look at the competition."

"Lord, the rumor mill in this town really does work even faster than the press."

"And they're probably more accurate too," Gabi says as she places cucumber slices over my eyes. "I've heard what the news said yesterday, and there's no way in hell your husband was a Riscoff. There's not enough money or liquor in the world to make me believe that."

I find it comforting that she doesn't actually ask me whether it's true.

"Anyhoo, enough of that and back to Maren. She's way more fun to gossip about. Although, I wouldn't want to face her without armor. Especially not when she thinks you're trespassing on her property."

"He's a man. Not land."

"And yet Maren will probably happily piss all over him."

I cringe. "Gross."

"Just saying, she's the kind of woman who'd do anything to secure her spot when it comes with a billion dollars attached."

"My cousin Cricket calls her Cuntcake McWhoreson."

Gabi bursts out laughing. "I knew I liked her."

AN HOUR AND A HALF LATER, my face is glowing, and I give Gabi a hug. "I don't know how long I'll be here, but I'll try to come back down at least one more time."

"I'm going to hold you to it, Whit. It's such a treat."

She leads me down the hallway, and I hear familiar giggles coming from a doorway up ahead. I pause when I see Karma and the girls all seated in pedicure chairs.

"Are you guys having fun?" I ask my little cousins, and the girls squeal their excitement. "What color did you pick?"

"I got pink!"

"Mine are purple."

They hold out their fingernails, and I move closer to inspect them.

"They look so pretty." I glance at Karma, and of course her resting bitch face is on point. "I hope you're all having a nice afternoon."

"We're trying," my cousin replies.

"I'm sure you'll take full advantage of the amenities while we're here."

"My kids are missing school, but at least they're finally getting what they deserve."

I give her a tight smile and leave the room as quickly as I entered.

As soon as we're out of earshot, Gabi asks, "What is her problem? She's always been such a bitch."

"I have no idea. But I'm not going to let her ruin my day." Karma's attitude is definitely what Magnus would consider a stormy cloud.

Gabi leaves me at the entrance to the women's lounge,

and I open the door to the locker room and run smack into a blonde. I bounce back.

"I'm sorry—"

"Oh. You."

Her tone and the look on her face give me the clues I need to figure out exactly who she is.

*Maren Higgins.*

# LINCOLN

EVER SINCE I left the resort this afternoon, I've been trying to find time to listen to Ricky Rango's songs, but the universe seems to be conspiring against me.

First, one of our logging crews had an accident, and I spent a few hours in the hospital making sure the guy who got hit by a snapped cable wasn't going to lose his hand. Thankfully, we have great doctors and surgeons on staff, and they all said he'd make a full recovery after surgery.

I hurried back to the office, just in time for legal to let me know that one of our customers has filed suit on a supply contract dispute.

And then, through it all, my mother left message after message.

When I finally have five minutes to myself, I return her call. It's either that or risk having her show up at my door, and that's the last thing I want to deal with.

"What did you tell them?" she says in lieu of a greeting, her tone sharp.

I know exactly what she's talking about, but playing dumb is obviously the best choice. "You're going to have to be more specific, Mother. Who did I tell what?"

"The household staff is acting strangely, my mobile phone has disappeared, and the internet is out. Your sister won't answer my calls, and your brother told me to ask you for an explanation."

Part of me is actually shocked that Harrison didn't take the opportunity to fill my mother in on every little detail. But then again, he's always been a coward, and he's probably afraid she'll kill the messenger. No doubt that's why he sent her to me. There's nothing my brother would love more than to give my mother another reason to despise me.

Unfortunately for Harrison, he's not going to get his way this time, because I'm going to kick the can down the road exactly the same way he did. Commodore is the one who's been withholding this information from us all for months, and he's going to be the one to break the news to my mother.

"Has Commodore been over?"

"Of course not," she snaps out. "You know that old man avoids coming here at all costs."

I don't respond to her comment because she's correct. Commodore moved out of the estate when he started feeling unwell . . . but not until he accused my mother of poisoning his morning coffee. Now, when he comes to the estate, he refuses to eat or drink anything he didn't personally bring with him. Obviously, I come by my trust issues genetically.

"I would expect him to stop by sometime tonight or tomorrow. Information has come to light that he'll need to share with you. And I'm sure your cell phone will show up and the internet will be fixed soon."

"What information? I want to know right now. I'm not waiting for that old dictator."

"I'm sorry, Mother. Commodore's orders."

"But—"

I disconnect the call and feel a twinge of guilt for all of two seconds that I hung up on my mother. I've already admitted I'm a shitty son, so it's not surprising. I've lost too many hours of my life to her tirades, and they never actually solve anything.

Letting Commodore take the role of explaining may seem like the coward's way out, but I'm not taking responsibility for the consequences of him sitting on the information for months. This could have been resolved easily enough if he had made different choices.

I rise from my chair and tuck my hands into my pockets as I walk toward the windows. The frothing water churns over the rocks, and I finally let myself ask the question I've been avoiding since yesterday morning.

*Was Ricky Rango my half brother?*

The very idea seems ludicrous.

I stride back to my computer and lean over it to type his name into the search bar.

Dozens of images pop up immediately. Rango onstage. Rango walking the red carpet. Rango on late-night shows, standing in front of exotic cars, signing autographs, and taking pictures with his arms slung around the shoulders of adoring fans.

I forget to look at his face for any kind of resemblance, because I'm too struck by one similarity all of the pictures share—Whitney isn't next to him in any of them.

I scan the screen, scrolling further down the page. Finally, at the bottom, I spot a photo where she's partially visible. It's another red carpet. Maybe some kind of awards show? She stares at the ground, a smile on her face that even I can tell is forced.

*She married him, but she was never happy with him.*

I've spent ten years assuming she was off living the high life as the wife of a rock star, but I've never been more wrong about anything.

No more assumptions when it comes to Whitney. *None.*

I lower myself into my chair and reach for my phone to listen to the songs she wrote, but it vibrates with a call as soon as I touch it.

*Commodore.*

"Yes, sir?"

"Meet me at the cemetery. Now."

# WHITNEY

"Excuse me. So sorry."

The blonde steps back. Her look of surprise is impossible to miss, as is the sharp knowledge in her gaze. She says nothing as she looks me up and down.

"They were right. You're here."

I decide that this is one of those times where it would behoove me to play dumb. "I'm sorry? Do I know you?"

Maren takes a step forward and gets a little too close for comfort, but I'm not about to step away. Women like her are the predators of the female gender, assessing potential prey for signs of weakness to determine who will be the easiest to attack. It's a behavior I may as well have a master's degree in after watching it so often around Ricky and his bandmates. When it comes to snagging rich and powerful men, women can be absolutely terrifying in their determination to win.

"*Do you know me?* Really, Whitney?" Her snide tone drips with condescension.

Instinct makes me straighten my shoulders and stand taller. *I'm not the weak one here today,* I remind myself. *I'm confident and strong.*

"I'm afraid you have me at a disadvantage, Ms. . . ."

"Higgins. Maren Higgins."

I keep my politely confused expression in place as I shake my head. Ricky wasn't the only good liar. I can pull it off when needed.

"I'm afraid I have no idea who you are. Which is strange . . . considering you seem to think you know exactly who I am. If you'll excuse me, I have somewhere else I need to be, and you're blocking the door."

She stays put, her mouth twisting in a way that's wildly unattractive. "You can pretend all you want, but we both know that you're here trying to steal *my boyfriend*, and I'm not about to let that happen."

"I think you've been misinformed, Ms. Higgins. I'm here because this town is my family's home. In fact, since you know exactly who I am, you know Gable is named after us."

"I don't care who it's named after. The Riscoffs own this town, and Lincoln Riscoff belongs to me. You need to back the hell off before I make you."

I should have known politeness wouldn't get me far with Maren, but at least I tried it. I really did. Now I'm done letting her sling threats at me without protecting myself. Women like Maren understand one language: bitch. And luckily, after ten years in LA married to a rock star, I'm fluent in the dialect of *super-sweet bitch.*

"Oh, *you're the fling.*" I impress myself with how

authentic my surprised tone comes out. "I did hear about you, actually. No one has ever called you a girlfriend, though. I was under the impression you had an on-again, off-again thing that has firmly been in the off position for a while."

Her back goes poker straight. "I don't know what he told you, but Lincoln and I are in a relationship."

"To be totally honest with you, Maren, Lincoln never mentioned you. I heard the gossip around town. You know how this place is."

She jabs her finger into my robe. "Listen up, bitch. He's mine."

This time I do step back, because I don't want her touching me.

"First off, don't ever touch me again. My lawyers would eat you alive in court. Second, you should probably clarify things with Lincoln if you're so sure he's your property."

Rage burns in her gaze, and I can see how badly she wants to shred me to pieces with her tongue and her claws, but she reels it in and steps back. Retreating to fight another day, no doubt.

Her expression turns into a creepy mask of calm to blanket the anger, and I realize I made an enemy in Maren Higgins long before this moment.

"It was nice to meet you, Whitney. Next time, I'll be sure to bring my card so if you ever want to move out of your aunt's shed, I can find you a place. Maybe the trailer park?"

I smile as sweetly as I'm capable. "Thank you so much for the offer, Maren, but I'm staying here at The Gables, and it's just too comfortable to consider wanting to leave anytime soon."

Her mouth pinches before she opens it to retaliate.

"Ms. Higgins?" A spa attendant stands in the doorway to the lounge. "I'm looking for a Ms. Higgins."

"I hope you enjoy your service, Maren. It was lovely to finally put a face to the gossip. Please don't take this the wrong way, but I hope I don't run into you again."

Maren's brows deepen into a *V* as she stalks around me, and I can't stop the victorious smile that spreads across my face.

*That's right, Maren. I might have been beaten down, but I'm still better at this game than you'll ever be.*

I move to the door to the locker room, but it's already open. McKinley Riscoff stands in the doorway with a grin on her face and starts a slow clap.

# LINCOLN

THE CEMETERY ISN'T my favorite place to go, but when Commodore hung up before I could reply and didn't answer when I called back, the choice was taken out of my hands.

He beat me here, which isn't surprising. I park behind his Escalade and climb out of my Range Rover. Commodore's power chair is parked on the paved path in front of the Riscoff mausoleum.

When I stop beside him, he starts speaking.

"I always expected I'd be in there long before now. Long before my son."

"I'm sorry, sir. None of us expected things to go the way they have."

He looks up at me. "Roosevelt passing before me actually made things easier, though, if you want to know the truth."

"What?"

Commodore lifts a hand to his face and brushes his

knuckles over his lips before he replies. "I didn't want to leave the company to him. I couldn't."

"What?" I hate to repeat myself, but the shock of his words has stolen any others from me.

"He couldn't and wouldn't protect and preserve the legacy. I knew that a long time ago." My grandfather glances up at me. "Why do you think I called you home that summer?"

My skin prickles, feeling two sizes too small for my body. "You knew then . . ."

"That your father was more worried about sneaking around on your mother than dedicating himself to the company I gave everything to build? Yes."

I lower myself onto a marble bench, trying to process the bomb he just dropped on me.

"I wanted time to groom you before I died, and I didn't know how long I would have," he continues. "The legacy has to be protected, no matter what it takes. My great-great-grandfather didn't trust his sons not to tear it apart to each take their own piece. So he adopted the English entailment mindset. The oldest son would get everything, and he would take care of everyone. But your father was only interested in taking care of himself. I couldn't take the risk that he would drain the bank accounts, sell off the assets, and run away with one of his women."

"Did he know that?"

Commodore looks off into the distance. "Yes. He knew. The day of the accident . . . we fought. I lost my temper. I told him he would get nothing from me."

My elbows drop to my knees and I clasp my hands

together. I lower my head to rest on my fist. "Jesus Christ. So that night . . ."

"He was leaving for good, and I knew it. I wasn't going to stop him. But instead . . . I killed him."

My stomach plummets as I look up at my grandfather. "You were there? The night of the accident?"

He shakes his head. "No. But I might as well have been. It was my decision that put his car on that bridge."

"Jesus fucking Christ. Why are you telling me this now?"

Commodore is quiet for several moments. "Because the sins of the past always come back to haunt us, and what you don't know can hurt you. I shouldn't have kept the paternity claim from you. That was a mistake, and now we have to do something about it."

"What do you want to do?"

My grandfather leans back in his chair and threads the fingers of both his hands together. He taps his thumbs, and I suspect that whatever he says next is going to change everything.

"This morning, my private investigator found a marriage license between my son and Renee Rango dated two years before he married your mother."

I stare at him in shock, barely able to grasp the implications of what he's saying. "When was the divorce?"

He presses his lips together, and my gut sinks lower. *No . . . he's not going to say what I think he's going to say . . .*

"As far as we can tell . . . there wasn't one."

# LINCOLN

*The past*

As impatient as I was to try to see Whitney again, I knew I needed to have all my facts together before I did.

For the last two days, I'd been on the phone with an investigator in LA who was compiling a report on Ricky Rango. Turned out, the motherfucker didn't just cheat on her once, he'd cheated on her multiple times. As the investigator reported back with each instance, it made me sick to my stomach.

I looked down at the notes I'd taken on my yellow pad, at the list of names and dates and places, and the truth hit me.

*I can't tell Whitney this. Not a single fucking bit of it.*

I shoved it away and sat back in my chair. I was in my office, because according to Commodore, life and business must both go on, no matter that we had a funeral tomorrow and my father was being buried.

The Gables were burying both of their parents on Saturday. It gutted me to think of Whitney at the grave site with Rango's cheating ass standing beside her.

At least she had her brother, no matter how much I didn't like the motherfucker. But if some guy was trying to come at McKinley under circumstances like this, I would do anything I could to keep him away. There was nothing I wouldn't do to keep my little sister safe, especially from a guy I thought had fucked her over.

And I had fucked Whitney over in my own way. I threw her out in the middle of the night. Barefoot. *Because I'm a stupid son of a bitch who couldn't trust her.*

Not even I could blame her if she didn't forgive me. I deserved to lose her, but I wasn't going to let it happen without a fight. Especially not to a piece of shit like Ricky Rango who deserved her even less. I glanced down at the lined yellow paper and all the instances of his cheating that had been documented.

*I won't let him keep me away from her. I won't let him win.*

I grabbed a new notepad and started writing Whitney a letter. Now I just had to figure out how to get it to her.

# WHITNEY

*Present day*

"I KNEW I LIKED YOU," McKinley says. "At first I thought you were the stoic, quiet type, but that was impressive."

My cheeks heat with embarrassment that someone witnessed our encounter. "I'm so sorry. I shouldn't have—"

"Put that bully of a woman in her place? Don't apologize on my account. That was long overdue, in my opinion. I've been terrified that Lincoln would somehow fall into her trap and not realize what she is before she conned a ring out of him. Besides, I'm the one who should apologize. You shouldn't have had to deal with her here. That's unacceptable."

"It's okay. I survived. She might think she's scary, but there's nothing that woman could say to me that hasn't already been said."

"Still, we promised you a safe haven, and I didn't live

up to that promise. I'll have her banned from the premises until further notice. She'll probably go crying to Lincoln about it . . ."

"That's really not necessary. She's a pest. She can't actually hurt me. I can easily avoid her in the future, now that I know to call down and check to see if she's on the books."

"How about I just tell the spa coordinators that when it comes to Maren Higgins, we have no appointments until otherwise instructed. They're already well aware of her freeloader ways. A couple months ago, she started coming in and trading on Lincoln's name to get free services, but I shut that down as quickly as possible."

Her comment about freeloading unleashes a rush of the guilt I've been storing up. "I don't want to be a freeloader either. This wasn't my idea, and we can move rooms or leave anytime. This isn't something I expected, and I truly don't intend for us to stay long, despite what I said to Maren."

McKinley waves me off. "Don't spend a single second worrying about it. Besides, I just told you I like you. I don't like many people, especially not the women who date my brother. And people I do like, I'm willing to do anything for. That's just the way it is."

"We're not dating," I say, trying to clarify something I don't totally understand myself.

Her brows rise, skepticism stamped on her features. "Either way, I like you, and you're welcome to stay. It's a rough time for both our families, so it's the least I can do."

"I'm sorry about your father," I say quietly. "I know yesterday was a hard day."

"For all of us. I'm sorry about your parents too." She pauses. "But whatever they did, it's not on us, and I wouldn't hold someone's actions against their child."

"Thank you." It's nice to feel like I have at least one supporter in the Riscoff family outside of Lincoln.

"Besides," McKinley adds. "You probably don't remember, but you stood up for me once when I was in middle school. Older boys were giving me a hard time, and you told them to leave me alone or your brother would beat them up. I never forgot that. Consider the rooms here my overdue thank-you, and truly, you're welcome to stay as long as you like."

---

I THANK Lincoln's sister again before locating my locker, and change out of my robe back into my street clothes.

Although this afternoon has been a little rocky, I feel pretty damn good overall. I refuse to let my run-in with Maren get me down. As far as I'm concerned, going forward, she doesn't exist in my world. *How's that for some positivity?*

When I make my way to the elevator bank, Karma and her girls are just entering one.

"Get in if you're going up. Otherwise, catch your own."

I still haven't solved the mystery of why my cousin is such a bitch, but I'm going to assume she just can't help it. Maybe she only sees the clouds. Either way, her attitude makes me want to redouble my efforts to follow Magnus's advice and change how I view the world.

"Can I see your nails?" I ask Maddy as I squat beside her, and she holds out her fingers. "Cute! Is pink your favorite color?"

"No," Karma says. "Her favorite color is blue, but this place is too classy to have that. Of course."

I cringe at the thought of Karma passing on her crappy attitude to these two precious little girls, but instead of saying something that will no doubt make the situation worse, I ignore her. This isn't the time or the place.

"Was it fun?" I ask the girls instead.

"Yes! They put bubbles in my water."

"My feet smell like peaches!" Addy lifts her foot into the air and almost tips over.

I steady her with a hug. "You both looked like princesses sitting there being pampered."

"They should," Karma says. "They are my little princesses."

"And Mommy says someday a prince is going to come take us away to live in a castle!"

"Princesses can build castles of their own too."

I have no idea where that came from, but as soon as I say it, I realize I mean it. I don't want these little girls thinking they need a man to give them what they want in life. They can get it for themselves.

"Whatever. Maybe in your fairy tale, but in this town, that's not how it works." Karma side-eyes me. "You didn't save yourself. We're only here because you're—" She cuts off what she was going to say, and I'm guessing it's because it's not appropriate for children.

"We're here!" Addy cheers as the door opens.

The girls race out of the elevator when they see Jackie

sitting in the lounge, and while they're distracted, I block Karma.

"I've never known what your problem was with me, and at this point, I don't care. But have you ever thought of checking your attitude around your girls? They don't need to hear or see that."

Her eyes narrow on me. "First, don't tell me how to raise my kids. You don't have any, and you don't know jack shit. Second, go fuck yourself." She knocks into my arm with her sharp elbow, and I step back.

Maybe I shouldn't have said anything, but her attitude seems to get worse by the day, and it's not just her mom and sister who have to deal with it anymore. Her kids are learning from her, and I would hate to see such sweet little girls end up as bitter as Karma.

I follow her toward Jackie, who has them both hugged tightly against her.

"You look so pretty! Did you have fun?" she asks as she releases them.

"We did!"

"They're tired. It's nap time." Karma grabs both girls by the hand and drags them back to the suite while Jackie and I stare after her.

When they disappear into the room, Jackie shakes her head. "I just don't know where I went wrong with her."

Since I have absolutely nothing helpful to say in response, I change the subject. "How did your first day with the new job go?"

The regret on Jackie's face fades away.

"Really good. Ms. Riscoff and I had a meeting this morning, and I spent the rest of the day training with my new boss." She lifts a champagne flute from the bar. "I'm out of the basement and working in the light."

"Congratulations. You look . . . *happy.*" And she does. Jackie's face seems to have lost five years, and the smile she's wearing is the biggest I've seen since I've been home.

"It feels good to be wanted. To have someone tell you that you're worth something and you're a valued part of the team." She pauses. "Thank you, Whit. I know this is all because of you, and I'm grateful."

I shake my head. "No. This is all because of *you.* You're the one who impressed the boss so much that she was willing to do anything to get you back. How do you feel about having a little celebratory dinner tonight?"

"Up here? Room service? Like we're fancy?"

The bartender sets a glass of champagne in front of me without me even having to ask.

I shoot a wink at my aunt. "There's no *like* about us being fancy. Clearly, we *are.*"

She lifts her glass and clinks the rim against mine. "Then by all means, we better celebrate. Who knows when we'll get another chance."

# LINCOLN

MY CONCENTRATION HAS BEEN TOTALLY SHOT since Commodore's nuclear bomb of a disclosure this afternoon. When I return to the office, I work late into the night to take care of everything that needs my attention, but I'm doing a half-assed job at best.

Commodore's PI is still working on finding a divorce decree or an annulment, but until he does, I have to face the possibility that my father was a bigamist, and all three of us are technically illegitimate.

*How the hell am I supposed to tell my mother? Or my brother and sister?*

I can't.

They can't know anything until we have more information. *No one* can know anything.

There's still something I can't figure out for the life of me. Why the hell would Renee Rango wait until now to push the paternity suit, and why hasn't she gone public with the fact that she was married to my father?

It makes absolutely no sense to me. Her motive has to be money, but her actions don't add up.

*What the fuck did you do, Dad?* The question has circled my brain a hundred times today, and I'm still no closer to coming up with an answer.

After another hour of attempting to be productive, I finally give up. I'm fucking useless tonight, and I recognize when it's time to quit.

I shut down my laptop and slide it into my briefcase. Even though I won't touch it again before morning, I won't risk leaving it here.

That's how much I don't trust my own brother, especially now.

When I walk out the door of the office, all I want is oblivion for one night so I can forget about what I learned this afternoon. I want to pretend for a few more hours that everything I thought I knew about my family hasn't shifted on its axis.

And I know exactly how I'd like to achieve that oblivion—with Whitney in my bed.

*I'd give every dollar in my bank account to have her.*

I laugh at the thought. Leave it to me to fall for the one woman I could never buy.

My plan to take it slow is working. Lunch was good. She gave me an ultimatum about a date, but that doesn't mean I can rush back to her room and push her up against the wall and take her the way I need to right now.

No. I can't do that until I win back her trust.

I'm no stranger to persistence and perseverance. She deserves both and more from me, and she'll get them.

But that doesn't stop me from thinking of the suite I

keep on the VIP floor for my own personal use. The press may still be camped outside my gate, and I don't want to deal with them tonight. Getting in last night was like running the gauntlet.

It's not like Whitney needs to know that I'm sleeping in the room beside hers. I can keep myself from stopping in front of her door and begging for what I really want from her.

I do have some self-control.

*Except when it comes to her . . .*

# WHITNEY

KARMA and the girls joined us for dinner on the terrace but headed to bed shortly after, even though the girls begged for dessert and I could tell Jackie wanted them to stay. But they're Karma's kids, so she bit her tongue.

To be honest, I wasn't sad to see the back of Karma because she spent half of dinner talking about how she couldn't believe I didn't go to my parents' graves yesterday on the anniversary of their death. Did I feel shitty about it? Absolutely. Was there anything I could change about how yesterday went? No.

Jackie's celebratory attitude faded as Karma hit me with jab after verbal jab, so as she left the table, I ordered two more bottles of champagne and every single dessert on the menu.

Splurging has never been the norm for me, even when I could afford it, but when it comes to making my aunt smile again tonight, I'm willing to do it.

When our majordomo knocks, I hop off the chair and

head for the door. Before I can open it, a second knock comes, along with a high-pitched female voice.

"Housekeeping. You want mint for pillow?"

I know that voice instantly, even with her fake accent, and I whip open the door.

"Cricket! What are you doing here? I thought you were laying low at Hunter's?"

She rushes in and wraps her arms around me. "And miss celebrating my mama's new job? Hell no!"

Jackie jumps up from her seat on the terrace. "You came!"

"I'm the good kid. When Mom calls, I come running."

Karma sticks her head out of the bedroom. "Keep it down. I have kids sleeping."

We all roll our eyes, and Cricket flips the bird in her sister's direction.

Thankfully, the majordomo arrives with dessert and champagne, and we close the doors to the terrace and restart our own little party.

"Hunter brought you?" Jackie asks.

"He sure did. Security is *nuts* here, even this late. They wouldn't let us through the gate until Hunter showed both our IDs. Apparently, you have to be on some magic list or you're shit out of luck."

"Wow. That sounds crazy."

Cricket tilts her head toward me. "The only thing that's crazy is Lincoln—about you."

"We're not talking about him tonight. This is about your mama."

"Damn right it is," Jackie says as she spoons up a bite of crème brûlée and pops a bite in her mouth. "I'm tasting every single one of these, and I don't give a shit if you judge me."

Cricket points at the strawberry tart. "As long as you save a bite of that one for me, I don't care. But first," she grabs the neck of a champagne bottle and lifts it from the ice, "we're cracking this baby open."

Being Cricket, she does the only thing I would expect from her, which is shake it up.

"Cri—"

But it's too late. The cork goes flying, and she sprays it over the edge of the balcony. I slap a hand over my mouth to quiet my scream so we don't attract Karma's bitchiness again.

Spray blows back on all three of us, and Jackie gasps. "Good Lord, girl. That's freezing."

Cricket drinks straight from the bottle. "But it tastes divine."

I catch a glimpse of the label. "It's like a grand a bottle, so it should."

Cricket chokes and smacks the bottle on the marble table. "Holy shit. We're fancy as fuck tonight."

I grab the champagne and fill our flutes. When I finish, I lift my glass in the air. "To Aunt Jackie. The hardest-working woman I know. The best role model. The best aunt."

"The best mom," Cricket interjects.

I nod. "And the best woman I've ever met. Cheers to you."

Tears shimmer in Jackie's eyes. "I love you girls so much." She holds out her arms, and Cricket and I both come toward her to be wrapped in a tight hug.

For the first time since I've been back in Gable, I know with one hundred percent certainty that I can't leave like I did before and not see my family for years at a time.

Moments like this are too precious.

---

CRICKET PASSES out on the couch after a call to Hunter telling him she doesn't need a ride. I slip out of Jackie's suite and tiptoe down the hall, a little tipsy.

As I wobble on my bare feet, I amend that thought. *A lot tipsy.*

When I reach the doorway to the pantry, a room filled with snacks and drinks for the use of guests, I pause. Gatorade is probably the only thing that's going to help me avoid a champagne hangover tomorrow.

I slip inside and fumble around in the dark until I find the flavor I want in the glass-fronted cooler. With the bottle clutched to my chest, I move toward the door.

That's when I hear footsteps coming down the marble hallway.

*Shit.*

The last thing I want is to run into another human being right now. I flatten my back against the wall and turn my head sideways so I can still see out the door.

It's a man.

A tall man.

A tall man with broad shoulders.

A tall man with broad shoulders *that I recognize.*

*Lincoln.*

Even drunk, I would know him anywhere. Hell, I'd

even recognize his *walk.* Confidence practically paves the way for each step. It's like he's never doubted a single thing in his entire life and can't imagine making a misstep.

I wonder what it would be like to be that sure of yourself. I also doubt I'll ever know, but I add it to my mental list of goals, anyway.

It doesn't occur to me to wonder what he's doing up here until his footsteps stop. I slide along the wall and peek out the doorway because I can't not look.

He faces a door at the end of the hall. My door.

*Lincoln came up here for me.*

I wait, barely breathing, because I need to know, and I'm afraid I'll give myself away.

Yet he doesn't do anything but stand there and stare at my door like he's having an internal debate.

I know all about those internal debates. Right now, I'm trying to decide whether I can keep quiet for another minute, because part of me—a big part—wants Lincoln to know that I'm watching him. Another part of me tells the big part to shut up because I can't be held responsible for what I would *do* to Lincoln if I he saw me right now. Probably climb him like a tree.

Finally, he reaches out, and my lungs freeze. *He's going to knock.*

But instead of curling his hand into a fist, he touches the door with his fingertips before turning toward the door adjacent to mine at the end of the hall. He waves a key card in front of the lock and disappears inside.

That's when it occurs to me. *Lincoln went into a suite on this floor and it's right next to mine.*

As soon as his door closes, I rush down the hall to let

myself into my room, and flatten my back against the door as soon as it closes. To my left in the sitting room, on the wall that separates my suite from the room he's in, is a locked door.

*A locked connecting door. To Lincoln's suite.*

I stare at it for several moments, wishing I had X-ray vision so I could see what he was doing beyond that wall.

Obviously, because that superpower eludes me, I close my eyes and use my imagination. Not so shockingly, it's even better when lubricated by champagne.

In my mind, I watch Lincoln shrug off his suit jacket and toss it over the back of a couch just like mine. He reaches up to his tanned throat to loosen his tie.

*God, ties are hot.* Someday, I want to pull it free from its knot and tease him with it.

But back to my fantasy.

His capable fingers work each button free and his white shirt falls open, revealing that muscled chest and hard stomach I didn't know he could still have ten years later. But he does. I know because I saw it. I might have been tipsy that night too, but the memory is burned into my brain for eternity.

He reaches for the button of his slacks and shucks them off. When he shoves down his boxer briefs, letting his big cock spring free, I can't stop myself from moaning at the mental picture and move closer to the connecting door. I lean against it, picturing Lincoln fisting his cock, and I slide my hand into my shorts.

As soon as my fingertips slide across my wetness, I groan and drop my head back. When it smacks hard against the wood, I freeze.

# LINCOLN

THE SOUND that comes from the connecting door has to be my imagination. There's no way Whitney could know that I'm in here. Even so, I pause in the act of pouring my drink and wait for another knock. All I hear is silence.

I set the decanter down and cross the room. I feel like an idiot as I put my ear against the panel.

Nothing.

My hand drops to the lock of its own accord and I twist it. The door, meant to allow for a VIP guest to reserve two suites and maintain privacy as they move between them, glides open.

Instead of seeing her face like I hoped, all I see is the white panel of the second door.

I listen closer, and I swear I can hear her breathing. Like I did minutes ago, I reach out and press my palm to the door.

Unfortunately, the fact that I want it to open doesn't magically make it so. I drop my hand, and my first instinct is to close the door as I back away, but I don't. Instead, I leave it open as I walk to the bar cart and finish pouring my drink.

After the day I've had, there may not be enough Scotch in this hotel to stop my brain from working, but I can try.

A shot of Whitney would do a hell of a lot better.

I take the glass back to the sofa and sit, but my attention stays on the door.

*Is she on the other side? Does she know that it took everything I had to stop myself from knocking?*

A minute later, I hear another noise. I bolt off the sofa and step closer.

At first, it sounds like a muffled voice. After a few seconds, I realize it's a *moan*.

"Whitney?" I say her name quietly, my mouth only inches away from the wood that separates us.

"I'm so close." She whispers the words just loud enough for me to hear them. My dick jumps against the silk lining of my suit pants.

"Open the door, Blue."

"That's a bad idea."

"I disagree. It's a fucking great idea."

She moans again, and all the blood in my head rushes south. I can picture her against the door, touching herself and writhing, and all I want is to see that firsthand.

"I just want to come . . . and then I'm going to bed."

"Even better. Now open the door, and I'll make that happen."

"Still a bad idea. You won't trust me in the morning."

A stab of guilt catches me, and it's one I deserve. "I promise that won't happen again."

Another groan filters through the door before I hear a thump.

"I want you. I do. I can't help it. But it never ends well."

I press my palm to the door. "Give me one more chance, and I'll prove to you that it never has to end at all."

# WHITNEY

LINCOLN'S VOICE, even through the wood, is way too dangerous to my composure. It's crumbling as we speak.

Everything I want tonight is on the other side of that door. It reminds me of that saying—*everything you want is on the other side of fear*. I think I actually have it printed on a T-shirt.

I fear what Lincoln makes me feel. I fear how things will undoubtedly fall apart. But even more, I fear never touching him again.

*"I'll prove to you that it never has to end at all."*

I've always said girls like me don't get happily-ever-afters, but my newfound positive streak shuts down the thought before it can populate in my brain. I kissed Lincoln today, and that didn't end in disaster. I laid down my stipulations, and he respected them. I even went up against that awful bitch Maren and came out the other side with a new Riscoff ally in McKinley.

*Good things are happening.*

Whether it's my outlook shifting or life finally going my way, everything seems to point in the direction of me flipping the lock, stepping beyond my fear, and taking what I want.

"Please open the door. You can slam it in my face again if you want in five minutes." He's not exactly begging, but I can hear the plea underlying his words.

He's right.

*I can be the one to end it whenever I want.*

Something about that realization sends a wave of power through me, and I unlock the door. I step aside as it swings open, and Lincoln stands there, suit jacket missing, tie loose, and his chest rising and falling like he just climbed twenty flights of stairs.

His gaze drops to where my fingertips are still caught in the waistband of my shorts.

"Fuck. Me. You were getting yourself off." It's a statement, not a question.

*Oh my God.* "Were you picturing me . . ."

Lincoln nods slowly, and I attempt a covert glance at his crotch.

The bulge is massive.

That wave of power whooshes through me again. "Were you going to . . ." My gaze dips to the bulge as I take a step forward. "Get yourself off thinking about me?"

"Damn right."

I take another step forward. "I want to watch you."

He reaches out to catch the loop on my shorts. With a gentle tug, he pulls me closer to him. "Is that right?"

"I was picturing you in my head. I'd rather see it for real."

He reaches for my hand, the one I still haven't both-ered to pull out of my shorts, and guides my fingers toward his mouth. "You were touching your sweet little pussy while you thought about me jacking off."

Shivers ripple over my skin, and my nipples tighten into even harder buds as he sucks each digit into his mouth.

"What if I want to taste you instead?" He scrapes his teeth along the pad of my finger, and it's on the tip of my tongue to agree to whatever he wants, but I find the strength to shake my head.

"I want to watch you first."

His hazel gaze heats. "Then that's what you're going to get."

With my hand tucked into his, he leads me toward the bedroom in a suite that's even larger than my own. I should probably ask why he's here, but I don't care enough to waste the time.

"Where do you want me, Blue?"

I don't hesitate to nod at the chaise in the bedroom. "Right there."

My breathing picks up as his lips curve, and he backs up until he's a foot away.

"Any other requests?"

I bite down on my lip, wondering if I really dare ask for everything I imagined in my fantasy. "Shirt and tie off. Don't sit yet."

My orders sound confident . . . because I feel it. Lincoln's following my commands. I'm in control. It's a heady feeling.

He pulls the tail of his tie free of the knot and holds it out like he's going to drop it on the floor.

"Throw it to me."

His Adam's apple bobs as he swallows. "What are you going to do with it?"

"Whatever I want."

His gaze heats further as he tosses it toward me.

I snag the tie out of the air and wrap it around my fist. "Now, strip."

Nostrils flaring, Lincoln undoes one button at a time, and I reach for the snap on my shorts. As he drops his shirt on the floor, I shove my shorts down my legs and kick them aside. Lincoln's teeth graze his lower lip as he reaches for his belt.

I settle on the bed, the tie slipping from my fingers as I get comfortable.

"If you touch yourself, I'm not gonna last long."

"You mean if I do this?" I slide my fingers into the waistband of my panties and let out a little gasp as they skim over my slickness.

"Fuck me," he says on a groan.

I shake my head. "Not right now. I'm busy."

Part of me can't believe the words that are coming out of my mouth, but I feel no shame. No embarrassment. Actually, the more his control shreds, the more powerful I feel. I'm calling the shots here.

Lincoln shoves down his zipper, and his cock bobs free of his pants.

My fantasy was wrong. There are no boxer briefs.

I drag my index finger over my clit, and my hips jerk at the spike of pleasure.

"Jesus, fuck. You're so goddamn sexy." Lincoln fists his cock and gives it a rough tug.

I put more pressure on my clit and demand, "Do that again."

Lincoln slowly jerks his shaft, and it's the hottest thing I've ever seen. I push two fingers inside myself and buck against my hand. His chest rises and falls as he watches me, lust practically rolling off him in waves.

"You look like you want to see more."

"Fuck, Blue. I want to see it all. Want to feel you. Touch you. Fill you up until you don't remember what it's like not to be full of my cock."

His dirty words unleash another rush of moisture between my legs.

"I'm so wet."

He squeezes his eyes shut as he gives himself another tug. A bead of pre-cum rolls off the head of his cock, and my tongue swipes along my lips.

*I want to taste.*

Lincoln's eyes snap open when I realize I said the words out loud instead of in my head.

"I want to give you everything you want, Blue. Just say the word."

I push another finger inside myself, but even that's not enough to fill me the way he will. I strum my clit harder and faster, and my orgasm builds.

"I want you to watch me make myself come while you stroke yourself."

His rough breathing is the only response he gives other than a nod.

I focus on his hand and the flex of his muscles as he works his cock, and I strum my clit. "I'm close. So close."

"Come for me. Come for me, and then tell me you want me to fill you up."

His order sends me over the edge, and I moan his name as the orgasm crashes down on me. "Hurry!"

He's off the sofa and beside me on the bed in seconds. "Trying to kill me. So goddamn beautiful when you come."

He shoves my panties aside, baring my fingers, which are still busy.

"I need you. Now."

The buzz of the orgasm fades away, and I want it back. I want exactly what Lincoln promised me.

"You've got me, Blue," he says as he comes over me, fitting the head of his cock against my entrance. "Always."

He drives home with a single thrust, and it's everything I need.

# WHITNEY

LIGHT SPILLS THROUGH THE WINDOWS, dragging me out of sleep. I blink a couple of times and remember where I am. The Gables. My suite. Except everything is in the opposite place it should be.

*Because it's not my suite. It's Lincoln's.*

I sit up, clutching the sheet to my chest. *Where is he?*

I scoot over to the side of the bed and my hand crushes a piece of paper. A note.

*I'm sorry you're waking up alone. I don't want to leave, but I have a meeting I can't miss. You're welcome to stay in the suite as long as you want, but I'm having something delivered to yours. I'll be back as soon as I can.*

*— L*

I READ IT AGAIN. *He's having something delivered?*

I wrap the sheet around my body and tiptoe out into the living room. I have no idea why I'm tiptoeing, but it feels like the right thing to do. The connecting door between our rooms is still wide open, and the events of last night come rolling back in vivid color.

*Everything you want is on the other side of fear.*

Once back in my room, I debate leaving the door open for several minutes, but I decide to close it just in case someone comes in and is predisposed to asking questions.

A half hour later, I've showered and ordered espresso.

The majordomo knocks, and I open the door wrapped in a fluffy white robe. But he doesn't just have my espresso. He also has a box on the tray that's the size of a ream of paper.

"Good morning, Ms. Gable. Mr. Riscoff thought you might need additional stationery for your room, along with some writing utensils."

My jaw slackens. *Lincoln sent me paper.* A sharp pang hits me in the chest but blooms into a cloud of warmth.

"Thank you," I say through the lump that has taken up residence in my throat.

"Of course. And if you need additional paper, pens, or anything else, please don't hesitate to ask. Also, if you've made your selections, I'm happy to take your breakfast order."

I rattle off something that I can't remember as soon as the request leaves my mouth because I'm too caught up in the paper that's now sitting on a tray on the desk. I whisper my thanks one more time before the majordomo disappears, and I stare at the box for long moments before my attention goes back to the door that leads to Lincoln's suite.

I open the box of stationery, grab the pen, and write a quick note to Lincoln. I slip back into his room, leave it on the matching desk, and hurry back out as though I'm more worried about being caught in there now than I was when I was ordering him to jack off for me so I could finger myself on his bed.

I can't wipe the secret smile off my face until I answer the knock on my door for breakfast.

———

AN HOUR LATER, after I've eaten my spinach-and-ham omelet, I decide to take advantage of the sunny day and lay out on the terrace.

*No clouds in the sky.*

Which is why I'm sweating within minutes and wishing I had a pool.

*Which I do.* All I have to do is leave my room and risk running into another human.

*Everything you want is on the other side of fear.* My mantra from last night echoes in my head.

Screw it. I load up my stuff and make the trek down the hallway, through the lounge, to the beautiful patio and crystal-blue water. Karma and the girls are nowhere to be seen, and neither is anyone else.

*See? That wasn't difficult at all.*

I choose a reclining lounger that's in the sun, but with an umbrella nearby, and lie on my stomach, jotting down words and phrases that mean nothing together. That's how my brain works. I write stream-of-consciousness style, putting whatever comes through my head onto paper, and then I piece it together like a puzzle when a pattern emerges.

I'm almost done with a chorus when another woman walks through the sliding glass doors in a black bikini and a turquoise blue caftan. Her face is shaded by a big floppy hat and large sunglasses.

I try to refocus on the paper, but my concentration slips again when she takes the chair directly next to mine.

She smiles and sets herself up, slathering her already golden-brown skin with sunscreen, and then pulls out a gossip magazine.

As soon as I see the cover, I cringe.

It must be a new one because the headline says WAS RICKY RANGO REALLY A BILLIONAIRE'S HEIR? The picture is Ricky onstage, overlaid on top of a photo of the Riscoff estate.

It's not a crappy gossip magazine either. It's one of the glossy ones I used to avoid looking at when I went through the checkout aisle at the grocery store. The story is too juicy for anyone to pass up.

As she flips the pages, my concentration and creativity dwindle to nothing.

*Not focusing on the clouds.*

I tuck my paper under my towel, ditch my sunglasses, and decide to go for a dip in the pool, carefully keeping my back to her and hoping like hell there are no pictures of me in that magazine.

I slip under the surface of the pool and push off the concrete with the soles of my feet, shooting forward underwater, my arms pulling me through. I try to make it all the way to the other end of the pool, but my lungs burn far too soon. Probably because it's been years since I last swam with any regularity. Regardless, when I resurface, I'm far enough away from her now. I let my body go limp and float to the surface, arching my back and soaking up the sun on my face.

I stay in the water, alternating between idly swimming laps and floating on my back, until my fingertips prune. With a glance toward my chair, I see the woman is still there, flipping through her magazine as she basks in the sun.

I pull myself out of the pool, letting the water stream off me, and grab a rolled towel from the rack near the stairs. After wrapping it around myself, I keep my face averted as I return to my seat and snatch up my glasses to put them back on before she can get a good look at my face.

"Gorgeous day, isn't it?" she says when I settle back onto the lounge chair.

"Definitely."

She must take my reply as an indication that I want to talk, because she launches into a conversation. "I love coming to places like this. It always feels so decadent when it's exclusive."

"Mm-hmm." I try to stop the chattiness, but she can't take the hint.

"Where are you from?" she asks.

"All over," I tell her, because I have no intention of telling her the truth.

"Ah, a citizen of the world. That's so fortunate. I'm a

born-and-bred Cali girl myself. It gets so stifling in the city, though. Everyone trying to outdo everyone else. It's nice to get out of there and appreciate different scenery."

"It's definitely different here."

"The Gables has been on my travel bucket list for years. I'm so glad I finally got to see it. What a beautiful place, right? And the food? To die for."

"Definitely." I pick up my paper and start writing again in the hopes that she'll get a clue and leave me the hell alone.

*Not so.*

"Have you been here before?"

I nod rather than answer verbally this time, and a rush of relief fills me as Karma and her girls come through the glass doors.

*Thank the Lord. I need a distraction.*

I wave at the girls and smile. "Hey! You guys ready for some swimming?"

"Yes!" Addy replies as she runs toward the pool.

"Addy, slow down. You're not getting into the pool yet."

"They're so cute. Friends of yours?" the woman asks.

"Yes." I keep my answer short, hoping she'll take the hint, not that it's worked so far.

Shockingly, Karma comes over toward me instead of heading to the opposite side of the pool. "Decided to finally risk leaving your room?"

I cringe. Maybe this was like wishing for a life ring and someone throws you one—but it's on fire.

"Thought I'd get some sun and swim."

"Hi, I'm Emmy." The woman beside me stands up and holds out her hand. "We were just chatting."

Karma eyes the lady and shakes her hand reluctantly. "Hi."

"Are you from here too? I was just about to ask your friend what I need to make sure I try before I leave town. I hear Gable has some pretty interesting history and infamous residents, past and present."

"Karma, the girls look excited to get in the pool. Do you want me to go swim with them?"

She shoots me a glare. "I don't need your help, *Whitney*."

The lady's kind smile turns into a grin. "And here I thought she'd never admit who she was."

Karma's eyes light up. "Who? Whitney Gable Rango? Yeah, that's definitely her."

I give my cousin the most intense side-eye I can possibly manage. "I think it's time for me to go now."

The woman reaches out and puts a hand on my arm as I stand. "Now, don't go running off just when things are getting interesting."

"Who are you and what do you want?" I drop any pretense of politeness.

"I could be your new best friend."

"I don't need any new friends," I tell her as I grasp my stationery to my chest.

"You really don't want to leave until you hear the proposition I've got for you."

"No, actually I do want to leave."

"I'm interested in what your new friend has to say,"

Karma says, and I want to smack the bitchiness right off her face. "Are you a reporter?"

Emmy nods with a smile.

"I don't know how you got up here, but you need to leave before security comes to show you out. That's the first call I make as soon as I step inside."

"Such a buzzkill, Whit."

"Shut up, Karma."

Emmy's eyes practically light up. "You two are just precious. My audience will love hearing about how Whitney Rango gets along with her family."

"How big of an audience?" Karma takes a step closer to her.

Instead of replying, the woman produces two business cards and hands one to Karma before shoving one at me. "Emmy Richards. *Daily Post*. I would love to talk to you, Whitney. I think your side of the story would be of great interest—"

"I'm not interested." I start to turn away, but she slips the card between my hand and the papers.

"You don't want to set the record straight? Tell everyone how you've been crucified in the press for causing Ricky's suicide when there's another reason he could've done it?"

"What other reason?" Karma asks, fanning the flames of this woman's ego.

"Don't you need to go watch your kids?" I ask my cousin, shooting a look toward the girls where they're both dipping their toes in the water.

"Leave my kids out of it. I want to hear what *Emmy* has to say."

"You're clearly the smart one in the family." Emmy speaks directly to Karma as if I'm not even here.

"Obviously."

"Did you know there's a rumor going around that your cousin's husband had a mistress and he really killed himself because of *her*?"

*Mistress?* I knew Ricky was cheating because of the STD, but I assumed it was some random skank and a back-stage hookup . . . not a relationship.

"What the hell are you talking about?" I demand.

Emmy turns her attention back to me. "I'm just saying that it seems like there was a lot more going on with your husband than you thought, Whitney. What if you could redeem yourself? Make his fans hate you a little less? Wouldn't that make life easier? I can help you do that, if you let me."

A tiny shred of my soul is tempted by her offer, but I know enough not to trust her or anything she says. "I'm calling security." I look at Karma. "You might want to take the girls back to the room so they don't have to see this."

She says nothing, just fingers Emmy's card and glances at me. "How much would you pay for a good story?"

"You can't be serious!" I step toward her and rip the card out of her hand.

"I'm not the one with a billionaire boyfriend. I've got two little girls to feed."

Emmy pulls another card from her purse and hands it to Karma. "Call me. We'll talk."

*Fuck. Now my cousin is going to sell me out to the press.*

# LINCOLN

*The past*

THE FUNERAL for Mr. and Mrs. Gable was a fraction of the size of my father's, even when it should arguably have been double, especially in a town named after their ancestors.

I saw Whitney dressed in black, walking into the church between her brother and her aunt. Even with her summer tan, her face looked pale, standing out against the dark dress.

I hated that I was watching from the other side of the street instead of holding her up and giving her strength to get through this day. That should have been my job, and I'd totally fucked it up.

I sat in a black sedan outside the church for hours, waiting for my chance. Finally, I spotted a girl with brown hair slipping out the side door. *Whitney's cousin.*

She was lighting up a joint when I got to her.

"Cricket, right?"

She looked up at me in surprise before giving me a short nod in response.

"Can you do me a massive favor?"

Her gaze narrowed. "What do you want?"

"I need you to give something to Whitney."

"Oh, really? Like what?" She flicked the ash off the end of the joint as I pulled the letter out of my pocket and held it out.

"Just . . . please give it to her. I need to see her. I have to talk to her. I swear to Christ I'll leave her alone if she tells me to herself."

Whitney's cousin studied me and took a drag before puffing the smoke in my face. A moment later, she reached out and snatched the letter from me. "Fine. But don't expect her to want to see you. She's already cozied up to Ricky like they were never apart."

"He doesn't fucking deserve her, and you know it."

Her shoulders dipped in a shrug. "I don't think you're the one who gets to make that choice."

The judgment in her eyes made me want to snatch the letter back, but it was too late. She shoved it in her purse.

"You should get out of here before Asa comes out. From what I heard, he's not your biggest fan."

"Just give her the letter."

She nodded, and I headed back to the car to watch the entire funeral procession leave the church, hoping for one more glimpse of Whitney.

# LINCOLN

I DIDN'T KNOW if she was coming. My watch showed that it was already fifteen minutes past the time I'd written in the note. I glanced out the window of the cabin again, and headlights cut through the darkness.

*Thank fuck. She's coming.*

As tires crunched gravel in the driveway, I hurried toward the door, pulling it open and rushing toward the car. I was two feet away when the driver's door flew open.

*It's not Whitney.*

"I told you to stay the fuck away from my sister." Asa Gable climbed out, his fists clenched and jaw set. Ricky Rango's head popped out of the passenger side.

*She got my letter and instead of coming herself . . . she told her brother and her boyfriend.* All the hope I'd been holding on to shattered. *She doesn't want to see me again.*

My teeth clenched and my entire body tensed as I accepted the truth.

"If she didn't want to come, she could've just ignored the letter. She didn't need to send you in her place. I would've gotten the message either way." I kept my tone flat, even though I felt like I was being shredded from the inside out.

Gable shook his head like he thought I was a dumb motherfucker. "She never got your letter, asshole, and if it's up to me, she'll never know about it."

His admission rocked me back on my heels and my jaw went slack.

*Her fucking cousin . . .*

Rango stepped up, cracking his knuckles. "Bad move, motherfucker. Karma sold your ass out."

"Karma?" I looked from Rango to Gable.

"Oh, you thought you gave it to Cricket?" Rango laughed. "Easy mistake since both those bitches look exactly alike."

"Ricky, don't call my cousins bitches." Gable stepped toward me. "I told you to leave my sister alone, and instead you try to draw her out here to the woods? You know what I have to say about that? *Fuck no. Ain't happening.* Not on my watch."

His boots crunched in the gravel as he stepped forward, flexing and clenching his hands.

I knew I was going to get my ass kicked tonight. It was on both their faces. They weren't leaving until they delivered a beating. I wouldn't go down without a fight, though.

"Just so you know, Gable, nothing you do to me will stop me from trying to get to her. *Nothing.*"

His grin carried no humor—only derision and violence. "I guess we'll see about that."

His fist flew out and caught me in the gut before the other busted open my cheekbone. I struck back with a combination, and he grunted as I connected. The Green Beret sent two more punches flying, one to my solar plexus and one to my liver, but I stayed on my feet, more than willing to trade. Then Rango jumped in, catching me in the side of the head before I realized he was moving.

Normally, two against one, I could hold my own . . . except when one of them was trained in hand-to-hand combat by Uncle Sam.

Gable didn't need Rango's help. He delivered a beat-down unlike one I'd ever experienced before.

I dropped to my knees as he landed punch after punch. I kept my guard up, swinging and missing over and over. He connected with a wicked uppercut to my jaw, and my body flew back onto the gravel. My fingers clawed the stones as I tried to push myself to my feet, but white spots dotted my vision. I couldn't focus and find my balance.

My ribs screamed as someone kicked me in the stomach.

"Get the fuck back, Ricky."

I blinked up to see Gable shoving his friend behind him. Whitney's brother stood over me, knuckles busted and blood dripping from his cut eyebrow.

"You learn your lesson yet, rich boy?"

"Go fuck yourself, Gable." I spat out a mouthful of blood.

He crouched beside me. "Watch your mouth or I'll bury you out here."

Before I could reply, another pair of headlights cut

157

through the darkness, and Rango squealed like a little bitch.

"Someone's coming! They'll fucking arrest us. I can't go to jail. My label will be pissed."

Gable looked around and spotted a two-track in the woods that led out to the field we hunted in. "Come on, we're out of here."

I pushed myself to my knees as they slammed the doors. The tires spun as they hauled ass around the side of the cabin.

The headlights of the newcomer stopped right in front of me, and I closed my eyes to avoid being blinded.

"Lincoln, that you? What the hell happened? You get robbed?" It was Commodore's voice. His footsteps crunched in the gravel as he came toward me. "Jesus fucking Christ. You got your ass kicked."

When I opened my eyes, the first thing I saw was his hand. I took it, and he pulled me to my feet.

Commodore looked over my shoulder in the direction Gable and Rango had gone. "Who was it? We'll bury them."

"I don't know, sir."

"Now, that's a damn lie and we both know it." My grandfather's brows dipped into an angry *V*. "This is about that Gable girl, isn't it?"

I said nothing, but Commodore didn't need me to tell him anything. He had it all figured out himself, just like he usually did.

"You can cover for that brother of hers all you want, but I'll still have him court-martialed for it."

As soon as he said *court-martialed*, my entire body

tensed. Any retaliation by Commodore would only succeed in making Whitney hate me more, and I couldn't let it happen. I straightened my shoulders and looked at my grandfather through the slit of my swollen left eye, since I couldn't open the right one.

"Sir, I respectfully request that you let me handle this myself."

My grandfather studied my busted face. "Give me one good reason."

I was silent for several moments while I thought of anything I could say that would persuade him. Finally, I went with the truth.

"I brought this on myself. I'm going to fix it myself too."

Commodore's eyes narrowed, and I could tell he wanted to argue. "Those Gable women are nothing but trouble. We know that. Don't repeat your mistakes. You're better off without her, boy." He jerked his chin toward the cabin. "Go inside and clean yourself up. Get some peas from the freezer for the swelling. I don't want to explain to your mother why you're going to have two black eyes tomorrow, so you'd better stay here until you heal up."

"Yes, sir."

Commodore took a deep breath and released it slowly. "If you change your mind, I've got the sheriff on speed dial. He'll have Asa Gable in cuffs before he makes it back to his aunt's house."

"Not necessary, sir."

He shook his head. "Come on. I need a drink. Your mother's wailing is driving me out of my goddamned mind."

I followed my grandfather into the cabin. Even though I was battered and bruised, body and pride, I still wasn't giving up. I would find a way to get to Whitney.

But I learned an important lesson tonight. *Don't trust anyone in the Gable family.*

# LINCOLN

*Present day*

"Security just removed a reporter from the VIP floor," McKinley says when I answer the phone.

"What?"

"You heard me. Whitney called it in. The woman was escorted off the premises."

I bolt from my chair and head for the door to my office. "Is she okay? Was she upset?"

"I haven't talked to her yet, brother dearest, only security. I imagine she wasn't thrilled, and neither am I. I don't know how the woman got through, but I'm going to find out."

"Fuck. I'm on my way over."

"Make sure you come in the back way; the front gates are a circus today. Before it was just press, but now there's a mob of angry fans out there with signs about Whitney. Someone definitely leaked that she's here."

"Shit. We're going to have to call in more help. If angry fans are here now . . ."

"They'll be all over town before long. I'm worried they'll try to vandalize Jackie Gable's house, so I'm sending more people over there too."

"Good idea."

I hang up with my sister and use my private exit to leave the office. I don't give a damn about the meetings and calls I'm going to miss this afternoon. They can be rescheduled. My only concern is Whitney—and the promise I broke.

I told her she'd be safe. I promised her she wouldn't have to worry because no one could get to her.

The ten minutes it takes me to drive, get through security, and get up to her room is ten minutes too long.

I knock on the door and wait, but there's no answer. I knock again.

"Blue, it's me. I'm so sorry."

The bolt turns, and she opens the door. Her dark hair is wet, and she's wrapped in a hotel robe.

"Why didn't you call me?" I ask her as she steps away from the door so I can enter.

"I handled it."

I want to shake her when she shrugs like it's no big deal.

"You shouldn't have had to handle it. Someone got to you, after I promised you were safe here."

Whitney swings her hair over her shoulder, and droplets splatter my shirt. "I don't think you get it. This isn't something you can make go away. People will always hunt down a story, and right now, that's me. You can't promise me that no bad things are going to happen, Lincoln. That's not how life works."

"How am I going to prove to you that you can trust me if I can't even follow through on that?" I step toward her and wrap my hands around the terrycloth covering her upper arms.

Whitney's blue gaze meets mine. "I should probably take a page out of the Riscoff family playbook and not trust anyone. Blood included."

"Please don't. You're better than that. Better than us."

She laughs. "I can't believe you said that with a straight face."

"It's the truth. Don't be like us. It's a habit that's fucking hard to break, and I'm working my ass off to prove to you that I have."

She's quiet for a moment. "I don't think I have a choice at this point. You know what my biggest worry is right now? Not that the press will get to me, but that my cousin is going to go to them."

It doesn't take a genius to figure out who she's talking about. *Fucking Karma.* I will never forget that she sold me out. I wouldn't trust her as far as I could throw her.

"Is there anything I can do?"

Whitney shakes her head. "Pray, maybe. But wait, it gets even better. And by better . . . I mean worse."

"What?"

"This reporter said Ricky had a mistress, and she dumped him at the same time I filed for divorce. She said that's why he killed himself. She wants me to tell my side of the story and exonerate myself."

"A mistress?"

She nods. "Apparently."

I search Whitney's face, trying to decide how she feels about this, but all I see is resignation. "You never suspected?"

"No. But I guess I should have. He fed me one pile of bullshit after another."

She looks up toward the ceiling, blinking back tears that make me wish Rango was alive so I could beat the hell out of him.

Whitney shakes her head with a sniffle. "I shouldn't even be surprised anymore. What kills me the most is that I'm trying so fucking hard to focus on the positive, but I know something worse is coming. I don't know what, but I feel it. Karma hates me. She's just waiting for her chance to do something awful, and I don't know how much more I can handle. All I want is some goddamn *peace* in my life, and I can't help feeling like that's never going to happen, no matter how hard I try."

Her body shakes as tears trail down her face. I hate hearing her sound so defeated, especially after the sexy display of confidence she showed last night.

I pull Whitney against me and wrap my arms around her. "You're going to have your peace. I swear to Christ, you'll have it, even if it's the last thing I do." I press my cheek to her hair.

"Don't say that. You can't make that promise either."

Her statement proves that she doesn't know me that well. "I can and I will. Starting with tomorrow night."

"What's tomorrow night?"

"You and me and Hunter and Cricket. We're going to have that dinner. Away from everyone. No press. No pressure. Just . . . peace." I tilt her chin up to meet my gaze. "Just say yes. I'll take care of the rest."

She stares at my face as though she's looking for answers, and I sure as hell hope she finds them. Because when I look into her eyes, I see everything I've ever wanted, and I'm not letting it slip away again.

Not this time.

Not ever again.

I lean forward and brush my lips across hers. "Say yes, Blue."

Her mouth opens, and I take the opportunity to deepen the kiss, tasting and teasing her. She moans softly, pressing her lips harder against mine as she meets me stroke for stroke.

When I pull back, her blue eyes are hazy with the same need that's pumping through my blood.

"Okay," she whispers. "Dinner tomorrow."

# LINCOLN

I'M MORE anxious than ever to get back to The Gables now that I have a plan, but my meeting with Commodore and the lawyers, minus the one who has now been fired for leaking information, is going longer than I expected. A meeting where we're talking about the easiest and quietest way to exhume my father's body isn't a conversation I ever expected to be having, but it's happening anyway.

"I think we should do it at night. No one will be the wiser."

Harrison rolls his eyes. "Like we're grave robbers? That's a respectful way to treat our father. Mother will never agree to it, anyway."

I don't know why Harrison is here, but Commodore wouldn't have invited him without a good reason. *Keep your enemies close*, I suppose. I hate that I have to view my own blood as a potential enemy, but Harrison doesn't leave me an alternative. After he missed the deadline for the auction bid, it seems clear he's deliberately sabotaging my efforts.

Commodore assesses Harrison. "Your mother will do what she's told to do." He glances at the lawyer. "I don't want to skulk around at night like we've got something to hide. It's already out. The press can report whatever it wants, and as long as no one is sharing information from the inner circle, we shouldn't have an issue." He doesn't look at Harrison when he says it, but we all know that's who he's talking to.

"I vote we have security and a barricade. Keep the press as far away as possible in the event they find out, and we can use a tent to shield what happens from the entrance of the mausoleum to the vehicle," Harrison says.

Commodore nods. "That's what we'll do then. Harrison, you're in charge of security and setup. Don't fuck it up."

My brother sputters, but Commodore is already rolling out of the conference room with the lawyers behind him before he can respond.

"Does he think I'm not capable of doing anything right?"

I look at him. "How'd that bid go for our acquisition?"

Harrison glares. "You think you're so fucking perfect? That you never fuck anything up? You're the one who turned this family into a joke ten years ago because of that Gable bitch, and now you're so fucking wrapped up in her again that you don't realize she's playing you."

I rise and place both hands on the table. "I may not be able to fire you, but I can damn sure beat the shit out of you. You want to keep talking?"

He goes silent, but the mutinous look never leaves his face. Harrison is up to something and I don't know what it is, but I'm going to find out.

But not right now. Right now, I have to finish arranging the most important date of my life, which is happening in a few hours.

Doubts about my sanity plague me as I stare at the clothes hanging in the closet of the suite.

*What was I thinking when I told him he could take me on a date?* That's right, I was riding that new wave of power and taking control of my life.

*Great plan, Whitney.*

I draw in a deep breath and exhale slowly.

*It doesn't matter what I wear. I'm not going to make a big deal about this.*

Then again, worrying about what to wear helps me put the million other things I've been stressing about out of my head. Like the reporter's number that Karma may have already used.

*Not thinking about that right now.*

Right now, I'm going to focus on the fact that I'm going on a normal double date. That's it. That's all.

Except I used to be in love with the guy, and every sign points to the universe conspiring to keep us apart. I still have a hard time believing that anything between us could possibly end well. Lincoln says it doesn't have to end, though, and as much as I want to believe that, the events of the past make it difficult, even with my newfound positive attitude.

His mother will never accept it.

He'll probably lose everything.

*Stop thinking about all the bad and focus on the good.* I snap out the order to myself and grab my phone to call Cricket.

"Hey, girl. I'm on a hike and I might lose you. Service is shit out here."

"What are you wearing tonight?" The question feels so normal and strangely good.

"Are you seriously asking me what I'm wearing on the mystery date? Who are you, and what have you done with Whitney?"

"It's either worry about clothes or the fact that your sister is probably selling my story to the press at this very moment."

"Fucking whore. You see why I didn't want her as my maid of honor? She'd probably try to nail Hunter in the closet and claim she was doing me a favor."

The sad part about this is that Cricket probably isn't wrong. *Great, a new worry to add to my list.*

"Clothes, Cricket. Let's focus."

"I don't know. A dress, maybe? You know if Lincoln's picking the place, it's going to be fancy as shit."

She's probably right.

"Can you make Hunter ask him where we're going?"

"What is this, middle school? Ask him yourself. He's your boyfriend."

"Lincoln Riscoff is not my boyfriend."

"Oh, so this is middle school, because you're denying the obvious. Have you not noticed that you're staying in a fancy penthouse suite, and it's all because of him? Oh, and then there's the fact that he's letting us get married at The Gables *for free* because of you."

Someone might have reached out of my closet and slapped me across the face for how shocked I am in that moment.

"What?"

"Hunter told me that Lincoln arranged it so there's no cost for *any of it.* Which means we get an open bar!"

Leave it to my cousin to be more worried about an open bar than the important point at hand.

"For free? Everything?"

"Hunter was pissed when he thought Lincoln was going to run you out of town, and Lincoln promised to fix it. Ergo, free wedding. Did I get that right? I've always wanted to say *ergo*."

Again, leave it to Cricket to get off topic.

"Why didn't Lincoln tell me any of this?"

"I don't know. You were probably too busy arguing or avoiding each other. Either way, I don't care because he can't take it back now, and Hunter's mom is off my back about them picking up the tab for the whole wedding and making me feel like I'm broke as a joke. Which I still am, but at least she can't shove it in my face as much anymore."

I stand in front of the closet in silence while I try to

make sense of all this. How I should feel about the fact that Lincoln is effectively absorbing the cost of my cousin's wedding.

"Whit? You there?"

Her whistle yanks me back to the conversation at hand.

"Yeah, sorry. I'm just . . . processing."

"I was surprised too, but I'm not letting him take it back. Which means you better wear something sexy that says you're going to put out tonight and won't look skanky in the morning when you have to put it back on again. Because if I had to guess, there's a one hundred percent chance of you getting laid in the forecast."

Cricket has no idea that Lincoln and I have already been down that road again, and with the connecting door, there's no need for concern about the walk of shame. That is, if he's still staying in that room tonight. *He could always stay in mine . . .* Part of me likes the idea of not being the one to sneak out in the morning.

"Okay, gonna lose you. See you at six. That's when he told us to be at the bar on your floor. You better not be late!"

Her phone cuts out, and she's gone.

*Six at the bar? We're having dinner up here?*

I think of Lincoln's promise that we wouldn't have to worry about the press, and I suppose that makes sense. He's going to close off the floor, and we'll have it all to ourselves.

But that's all way less important than the fact that he's *paying for my cousin's wedding.* Yes, Hunter is his best friend, but Lincoln wasn't paying for their wedding *before* I came back into the picture. What the hell does that mean?

I toss my phone on the bed and go back to staring at the closet. I don't know what to think about anything when it comes to Lincoln, so I try to worry about the one thing I can control—what I wear.

I grab a black wrap blouse, a pair of white linen pants, and cute strappy flats.

Done.

Simple.

Classy.

I glance over at the phone and wonder how hard I want to look like I'm trying . . .

*Screw it.* I need all the confidence I can get tonight.

Three minutes later, I have Gabi's assurance she'll be up at four, and I'm going to look like I didn't try at all to be drop-dead gorgeous.

Cricket was definitely right about one thing. There's no chance I'm going to bed alone tonight.

# LINCOLN

"Are you shitting me? You have got to be shitting me! That's a helicopter." Cricket stares at the chopper on the roof as Hunter pulls her against his side.

"He's not shitting you, babe." Hunter glances over his shoulder at me with an eyebrow raised, but I'm not worried about responding to him. All I care about is Whitney's reaction.

Her glossy pink lips are pressed together, and her gorgeous blue eyes dart back and forth between the chopper and me.

"Really?" she says, just loud enough to be heard over the quieting engine.

"Problem?"

She straightens her shoulders and lifts her chin, smiling at me. "I guess it'll do."

As Whitney walks toward the helicopter, my eyes are glued to her ass in those white linen pants. *Sweet fucking Christ.*

I hurry after her and help her into the bird. "You've flown in one before, I take it?"

"A few times."

For some reason, it pisses me off that I'm not able to give her a first because she's already done and seen so much. Then again . . . I think about the place I picked for our date, and after what she said about going places but not really experiencing them, I'm pretty confident tonight will be at least one thing she's never done. Hell, I've never done it either, and it took me over twenty-four hours and a lot of favors to pull it off.

Cricket and Hunter climb into the seat that faces us, and Cricket is practically bouncing as Hunter helps her with her harness. From the smile on his face, I might actually have redeemed myself with my friend.

Whitney has her harness buckled before I can offer assistance.

"Everyone ready?" the pilot asks.

As soon as I give the word, the rotors start.

"Where are we going?" Cricket asks over the noise.

I point to the headset. "Put it on so you can talk."

Hunter grabs both of them and positions one on her head.

"Where are we going?" Cricket repeats herself.

I glance at Whitney. "It's a surprise." Her brows go up. "Don't worry, I think you're going to like it."

I HAVE ABSOLUTELY no idea where Lincoln's taking us, and I'm not sure how I feel about surprises. Ricky never bothered to do anything special unless it was something for himself, but I have a feeling that Lincoln has pulled out all the stops to set up whatever is happening tonight.

As we lift off the roof, it's impossible to tamp down the excitement buzzing through my veins. Maybe I do like surprises after all.

The pilot's voice comes over the headsets as he speaks to the tower, and as soon as he goes quiet, Cricket claps her hands.

"This is so cool!" Her voice is high-pitched in my ear.

One thing is for sure—Lincoln scores extra points for making my cousin so happy. I hate that me coming home for her wedding has turned into such a disaster, but Cricket would never hold it against me.

Karma, on the other hand . . . All I can picture is her on the phone, telling that reporter as many horrible, embarrassing things as she could. After Lincoln left my room, I told Aunt Jackie everything that had happened, including about Karma taking the woman's card. Jackie promised she'd talk to her and would do everything she could to make sure Karma didn't call her.

"You okay?" Lincoln asks.

I nod and force all thoughts of Karma and the press from my mind. *Tonight, I'm going to relax and enjoy and not worry.*

Lincoln gestures out the window. "Isn't it beautiful?"

I look through the glass, and the gorgeous view of the river and mountains from above takes my mind off the chaos swirling inside me.

It's epic. The perfect moment to just *be*. Maybe even the perfect moment to find the peace I've been searching for.

I lose track of time of how long we're in the air as I soak up the gorgeous scenery beyond the chopper.

Mountains, forests, rivers, and lakes roll out below us, along with the occasional little towns. We swoop so low over one peak, I see animals galloping.

"Are those horses?" I point, and Lincoln slides his right arm around my shoulders and leans over me to look. My entire body buzzes to life as soon as his skin touches mine.

"Wild horses."

"Oh my God!" Cricket squeals and practically climbs over Hunter to see. "That's amazing!"

For the rest of our flight, Lincoln's arm stays around me, and I'm hyperaware of every shift of his body and flex of his muscles. It's the way I've always been around him.

That's never gone away, and part of me is starting to believe that it never will.

*Which only works if Lincoln is right and this never ends.*

I'm still not ready to believe that yet. It's too big and scary with massive potential for gut-wrenching disappointment. Even now, my stomach twists at the thought of losing him.

*Because I'm failing at not falling for him again.*

Before I can consider the implications of that thought, the ocean comes into view beyond massive cliffs. Rock formations dot the coastline, interspersed with small stretches of sand. It's absolutely incredible.

"Wow." I whisper the word, but of course, with the boom of the microphone near my mouth, everyone hears me, including Lincoln.

His hand closes around my arm. "Never gets old, does it?"

I shake my head, chancing a glance over my shoulder. My lips are only inches from his, and if my cousin wasn't clapping and squealing a foot away from me, I'd take the kiss they're offering.

"It never will," I say instead, and Lincoln's hazel gaze flares with heat. He understands what I'm saying.

His hand curls around mine as the chopper turns and flies along the cliffs for a few minutes until I spot a wider stretch of beach up ahead. A white tent is in the distance, probably our destination. But where the hell are we going to touch down?

I look around for some kind of cement pad, but there's

nothing but cliffs and wooden stairs leading down to the beach.

"Where is he going to land?" I ask.

"You'll see," Lincoln says as he squeezes my hand.

Cricket's eyes are as wide as I've ever seen them as the chopper starts to descend.

"Here?"

Lincoln nods as the pilot speaks in what sounds like code and gets the okay for landing.

My eyes widen as the chopper descends, and I realize it's not a regular beach we're landing on. We touch down on what looks like a million colored jewels—not sand. The pilot cuts the engine and the rotors wind down.

"Where are we?"

"A glass beach. It's not well known like some of the others, which is why the glass is still here. They dumped trash over the cliffs all along here in the early 1900s. Thousands of glass bottles were tossed over, and the waves took care of the rest."

My mouth hangs open in wonder. "I've never seen anything like it in my life."

Lincoln squeezes my hand. "A friend of a friend owns this stretch and agreed to let us land here and have dinner."

Cricket whips off her headset. "Can we get out? Is it safe? I've got to see this up close."

"Go for it."

Hunter opens the door of the helicopter, and Cricket is on the ground before I can even reach the buckle on my harness. Hunter follows her out but pauses in the doorway. "Thank you, man. This is incredible."

"He's right. This is absolutely incredible." I drag my

gaze back to Lincoln's face and stare at him with just as much wonder as I did at the beach. "I can't believe you did this all for us."

"Eventually, you're going to realize there's nothing I wouldn't do for you."

Lincoln's eyes are soft and filled with emotion I'm afraid to name. Warmth builds in my chest, and my grip on his hand tightens.

"Thank you for doing this," I whisper as I release his hand so we can both unbuckle our harnesses.

"No thanks necessary. I do have a question for you, though."

My entire body tenses. "What kind of question?"

"An easy one, I hope." Lincoln holds out his hand again. "Ms. Gable, would you do me the honor of walking on the beach with me before dinner?"

A smile stretches across my lips. "Yes, Mr. Riscoff. I would love to walk with you on the beach."

I reach out and slide my fingers into his.

# LINCOLN

JUST SITTING next to her during the flight made my night. But as soon as we're out of the chopper and on the ground, the look of wonder on Whitney's face is everything I've ever wanted to see there.

As soon as her sandals touch the beach, she whispers, "This is unreal."

I reach down and pick up a handful of colored glass that's been battered by the ocean and rocks until the edges are smooth and the glass is frosted.

"Hold out your hand." She does, and I drop the rainbow of sea glass into it. "So, what do you think?"

Whitney's chin jerks up toward me. "This is amazing. And absolutely nothing like what I expected."

"What did you expect?"

She laughs. "I probably shouldn't tell you . . ."

"Come on . . ."

"As soon as I saw the chopper, I figured we'd be going

to a swanky restaurant with a helipad on top that you bought out for the night so no one could bother us."

"I thought about it."

She stands, clutching what looks like a fistful of gems. "Why didn't you?"

"I figured you saw the inside of plenty of restaurants while you were seeing hotels and venues. I wanted to give you something different. An experience. I was betting you hadn't seen anything like this before."

Her lips press together and she closes her eyes for a beat. When she opens them again, her blue eyes shine. "You're right. I've never experienced anything like this before. *Ever.* This . . . this is special."

When she sniffles, I hope like hell I didn't make her cry.

Whitney turns away and drops my hand to gather up scoops of glass. "It's magical," she says as she lets the pieces slip through her fingers.

I want to tell her that anywhere she is would be magical, but I don't. "I'm glad you like it."

Her smile turns lopsided.

"Like it? We love it," Cricket yells as she trots down the beach. "This is fucking awesome!" She jumps into Hunter's arms, and he swings her around.

Whitney's smile grows bigger as she watches her cousin. After a few beats, she steps closer to me. "Thank you for letting me share this with her. It makes it even more special."

She lifts her mouth to mine and presses a kiss against my lips. It's brief and soft, but from Whitney, it's everything.

My goals in life shift as another one is added to the list. *Get her to kiss me like that again.*

Lincoln and I walk the beach, exploring and marveling at the smooth sea glass where there would usually be sand. I lose track of time as I soak up every moment of this experience . . . including the sense of peace that has settled over me.

It's the greatest gift anyone has ever given me.

What could have been twenty minutes or two hours later, my stomach rumbles.

"Would you like to have dinner now?" Lincoln asks. "It's ready and waiting for us anytime we want."

He hasn't left my side since we touched down on this incredible place, and since Cricket and Hunter went the other way down the beach, we've had complete privacy.

I glance in their direction and see both Cricket and Hunter holding drinks near the white tent as she points down and grabs another piece of glass from the beach.

"I could be talked into dinner."

He holds out his hand, which I've held on and off all evening, and sliding mine into it feels so *right*. Like this is the hand that was meant to hold mine.

It's been so long since anything in my life flowed easily without having to maneuver around a million obstacles, but tonight has been effortless. *I could get used to this so easily.* The thought doesn't even scare me as much as it did when we landed.

"I hope you like shish kebabs. I decided to keep it simple, but hopefully delicious."

"That sounds perfect." As we walk toward the white tent, I confess. "I totally thought you would pick some Michelin-star restaurant where Cricket wouldn't know which fork to use and feel awkward. And of course, the food would be gorgeous, but we'd all leave starving."

He glances down at me. "Is that really what you think about me? Because, if you recall, we did meet in a hole-in-the-wall bar where they pretty much sold just beer and tequila."

"I figured a lot has changed in the last decade."

"Some things. Not everything."

The look he gives me speaks volumes, and I want to ask *what else hasn't changed?* But I can't manage to get it out.

"You went to a lot of trouble tonight," I say instead.

"You're worth all this and so much more, Whitney. I won't stop until I prove it to you."

"IF I EAT ANOTHER KEBAB, I think I'm going to burst," Cricket says as she stuffs one last piece of grilled shrimp in her mouth.

The food was incredible, and I'm still glowing from Lincoln's words when we walked on the beach. Everything he's done tonight has made me feel valued and cherished. It's not a feeling I'm used to, but it's one that I'm going to hold on to for as long as I can.

I stab into one more piece of lobster and pop it into my mouth as the sun paints the sky with swaths of orange, red, and pink. There's truly nothing I would change about this night. Everything about it has been absolutely wonderful.

I finally push my plate away. "I'm done too. Everything was seriously amazing."

Lincoln smiles at me. "Don't tell me you didn't save room for dessert."

"Give me ten minutes. I can rally," Cricket says. "I've never said no to dessert."

Hunter laughs. "That's a true statement."

"I think we should have shish kebabs for our wedding reception, babe. I mean, if your mom wouldn't lose her mind over it, it would be the coolest thing ever."

Cricket's fiancé wraps his arm around her. "You can have whatever you want. It's our wedding. Not hers."

"The chef at The Gables will make you anything you choose," Lincoln adds.

"I still can't thank you enough for letting us have it there for free. Hunter keeps telling me it doesn't matter that Mom can't afford to pitch in much, but it was slowly killing me to let him pay for everything."

Hunter's face falls as he watches my cousin. "Baby, you know I don't care."

Cricket's shoulders tense. "But I do." She glances at Lincoln. "I know you're only doing this for Whitney's sake, but I want you to know I appreciate it like crazy. If you ever need good weed or a guided hike through the wilderness, I'm your girl."

My cousin's offer of marijuana as repayment breaks the growing tension.

"It's no trouble at all," Lincoln says with a laugh.

I reach out and lay my hand on Lincoln's thigh, and he stiffens, glancing down at it. "I appreciate it too. More than you know. Thank you."

His hand covers mine, and everything about it feels so right.

Hunter rises from the table, holding out his hand to Cricket. "Babe, let's take a walk and find you that red glass you've been looking for before the sun's completely gone."

My cousin hops out of her seat. "Yes! I'm not leaving without a red piece."

They head down in the direction that Lincoln and I walked earlier.

"You heard her," I tell him. "We'd better find her some red glass, or she'll literally camp out here until she finds it."

He helps me out of my chair. "I wish I would've thought of camping supplies. Next time."

"Next time, huh?"

Lincoln lowers our clasped hands until my body

presses against his. His lips skim across mine in a perfect kiss. "I've got ten years of dates to make up for. I'm just getting started, Blue."

*I could definitely get used to this.*

# LINCOLN

As the remnants of the sunset fade, we roast marshmallows over a bonfire and make s'mores, which turns out to be another right choice. It's simple, easy, and fun, which is exactly how I want to end the night.

Well, this part of it, anyway. When we get back to The Gables, I plan on spending hours making Whitney scream my name as she comes. This is the new beginning we should have had before, and nothing is going to stop me from making it perfect.

When we finally leave the beach, I have exactly one piece of glass. A bright blue one, the same color as Whitney's eyes. Whitney has a rainbow, and Cricket has Hunter's pockets bulging—including the red piece that it took all four of us looking for until the sun went down. I wouldn't have complained if it took all night, though.

Anything for more time with Whitney when she's smiling and laughing and *happy.* It's everything I wanted to give her.

The flight back to The Gables seems much too short, and the familiar cliffs are in sight when my phone buzzes in my pocket.

I pull it out to read the text.

MCKINLEY: *Mom knows about the Rango estate. She's on her way to the resort.*

"FUCK."

Everyone in the helicopter turns to look at me, and I realize I spoke into the headset.

"What's wrong?" Whitney's posture stiffens, which pisses me off even more because reality is the last thing I wanted to intrude on our evening.

And now hell is about to be unleashed because my mother has learned that Ricky Rango's estate is claiming he was my father's son.

*Thank God there's no way she could know that he might be my father's only legitimate son . . .* I lock that thought away because there's no way in hell I'm going to share the possibility.

"My mother found out about the paternity claim. We've been keeping it from her."

"Shit," Cricket whispers. "Only Ricky Rango could fuck things up this effectively from the grave. That takes some serious skill. If he were still alive, I'd kill him myself."

Cricket isn't the only one with that thought.

Whitney's hand squeezes mine, her eyes full of sympathy. "I'm so sorry. I wish this wasn't happening."

"It's not your fault. You literally had nothing to do with this at all. My father got my family into this mess."

As soon as I mention my father, she looks away, and I wish I hadn't. *Because he fucked up all our lives.*

We're all silent as the chopper finally touches down on the rooftop helipad at the resort. I thank the pilot before climbing out and helping Whitney. Hunter and Cricket follow us down the stairs that will take us back to the VIP floor.

As soon as I open the door to exit the stairwell, my mother spots us and marches toward me, a militant glint in her eye.

"We're gonna go," Hunter says. "Thank you, man."

I give him a nod. "Sorry about this."

"Don't worry about it."

He and Cricket turn and walk down the hall toward my mother. But she doesn't spare them a glance as she stalks toward me, fire and fury in her every step.

She points her finger at Whitney. "You put him up to this, you little whore, didn't you?"

I pull Whitney against my side, wanting to protect her from my mother's rage. "She didn't know anything about it."

My mother's gaze cuts to mine. "She's a liar! They're all liars! Every single one of those Gable whores."

"Mother—" I attempt to interrupt, but she's on a roll.

"Why else would she have married that Rango boy? You don't think I see how this all went down? She *knew* his dirty secret, and she couldn't get the Riscoff money through you, so she went after the next best thing. She *knew*!"

Whitney sputters beside me, but I'm not going to make her defend herself. Not now and never again. I don't care that the accuser is my own mother.

"That's where you're wrong. She could have had every single cent through me, Mother. She didn't need to marry him to get anything."

My mother gasps and slaps a hand to her chest, but I know if the revelation about the paternity suit didn't trigger an episode, this one is bullshit.

"Don't try to pretend it's your heart. I'm not falling for it this time."

Her face screws up into a pissed-off glare. "How dare you say I'm pretending!"

"You've been using your *heart condition* to manipulate us for years. It's not going to work anymore."

She gasps. "See! She's turning you against me. That's exactly what she wants. She wants to drive a wedge into the heart of this family and tear us apart."

Whitney sucks in a breath, and I press her tighter to my side. "No, Mother. You've managed to do that all by yourself."

My mother's eyes narrow. "It's time to choose. Her, or your family." Her gaze cuts to Whitney. "I hope you're happy about what you've done. You couldn't stay away. You had to tear us all apart, just like your mother."

Whitney tries to pull away from me, but I keep my arm locked around her. I'm not letting her go again.

"You want me to choose, Mother? I will."

# WHITNEY

MRS. RISCOFF'S words are shredding my soul. Somehow, I knew it would come to this. I knew she would make it an either-or situation. She could never let Lincoln and me be together.

I can't let him choose between us. I can't be the reason a family is torn apart. My mother already did that, and I refuse to do the same.

"Stop. Both of you." I jerk away from Lincoln's side so I can turn and see his face.

"Whitney."

"No, just listen to me for a minute." I hate how my voice shakes, but that doesn't stop me from saying what I need to say. "You only get one mother. Maybe you don't appreciate her now, and maybe you have differences, but you only get *one*." Tears fill my eyes. "I would do anything to have another day with my mom. *Anything*. I didn't realize how important she was before I lost her, and

I won't let you do this. I won't be the one who comes between you."

"Blue—"

Lincoln's brow creases with the same pain that's tearing me apart, but I know I'm doing the right thing. There is no other alternative.

"No. I won't let you choose between us, Lincoln. I can't be responsible for that decision."

I shake my head as tears track down my face. I was doing so great at being positive and looking at the future with hope, but I should have known better. That's not how things work for me.

I swallow, finding the strength to say this last part, and meet Lincoln's anguished hazel gaze. "I'll leave before I'll let you choose. I never should have come back. All I've done is cause pain for the people I care about. I'm done. I'm gone."

"Whitney, no. You can't—" He reaches out to grasp my wrist, but I snatch it back.

"I'm sorry. You should take your mom home. Spend time with your family. That's what matters. Not me."

He reaches for me again, but I shake off his hold and turn to walk away, trying to keep my head high as my tears fall faster and faster. Lincoln calls out my name and I break into a run, not stopping until I'm in my room with both doors locked.

I drop onto the sofa and curl into a ball. I knew I shouldn't have come back to Gable. I knew I shouldn't have ever looked at Lincoln Riscoff again. I knew I shouldn't let myself imagine any kind of happily ever after. All I've done is destroy more lives.

But I'm done with that. I'm done with all of it.

# LINCOLN

As I STARE in the direction Whitney ran, my heart cracks open in my chest.

"You have your answer. She doesn't want you, Lincoln. She's never actually wanted *you*. It's always been about what you could do for her."

I whip around to face my mother. "You don't know that."

"Then why did she marry that boy? Because she knew he was the heir, and she thought he'd inherit everything. She never loved you. She never wanted you. If she did, she would've walked away from him and stayed with you, even if it meant you got nothing. But she didn't. Those Gable whores only want the man that comes with the money. Why do you think she came back now?"

My mother's poisonous words seep into the part of me that always wondered how Whitney could have walked down the aisle to another man if she loved me.

"Are you willing to throw away your family for someone like that?"

With every jab, my mother thinks she's turning me to her way of thinking, but all she's doing is making me question *her*.

"What do you mean she would've stayed, even though she knew it would mean I inherited nothing if I chose her?"

My mother lifts her chin but doesn't answer.

"You got to her then years ago, didn't you? What did you say to her, Mother?"

Her jaw tightens, and I know my suspicions are right. My mother did something to push Whitney down the aisle to Rango, and I need to know exactly what the hell she did.

"Mother, you'll answer my question, or I'll make sure Commodore cuts you off without a dime."

Instead of replying, my mother turns on her heel and stalks down the hall.

*Oh, fuck no. I'm going to get my answers.*

But first—I need to talk to Whitney.

# WHITNEY

*The past*

CRICKET WOULDN'T TAKE no for an answer this time. She was determined to get me out of the house and back into the land of the living. Finally, she resorted to playing dirty —she bribed me with passion-fruit gelato from Tutti Frutti, and the fact that the owner told her she was almost out and wouldn't be making more for months.

I didn't even know what passion fruit actually looked like, but the gelato was pretty much the best thing I'd ever tasted in my entire life.

"Can't you bring some home to me?"

"It'll start melting, and then I'll have to lick up the drips, and before you know it, the whole thing will be in my belly."

I narrowed my gaze at my cousin. "And why can't you get it in a cup so it's not a big deal if it drips?"

She rolled her eyes. "I'm not bringing it to you. You

have to leave the house. You're starting to blend into the furniture, and it's not healthy. Go take a shower. Wash your ass, put on some clean clothes, and at least pretend you're still a functioning human being. You never know what'll happen—you might actually start functioning again."

The cracked pieces inside me threatened to shatter. Over gelato.

"I just buried both of my parents. Can't you bring me some freaking ice cream?" My voice rose until it was nearly a shriek at the end.

Cricket rushed toward me and wrapped me in a hug. "Jesus. Finally. Scream at me. Yell at me. Do something other than sit there like a mute."

Tears streaked down my face as my shoulders shook. "Why?"

"Because you're trying to bury yourself with them, and I can't let you do that." She sniffled. "I'm sorry, Whit. I don't want to make you cry, but I need you to stop staring through me like I'm not even here. I just want my cousin back, even if it's just a little. I need you to try to live again."

I knew what Cricket was doing, and I couldn't hate her for it. I let my tears soak her shoulder. But it was her sniffles and the tears sliding down her cheeks that made my decision easy.

"Fine. You win. I'll take a shower, and we can go get gelato."

She pulled back, blinking her bloodshot eyes. "Thank you, Whit. I know you won't regret it."

I hoped she was right.

AN HOUR LATER, Cricket and I were in Aunt Jackie's car heading downtown.

We parked on the street and climbed out. She didn't lie to me about the gelato, because I could see the owner waving and pointing at it through the front window of Tutti Frutti as soon as she caught sight of us.

Once I had a cone in hand, Cricket and I walked outside and wandered down Bridge Street toward the city square where there were benches in an area near all the little shops that seemed to be springing up one after another.

"Oh, do you see that dress? How cute is that?" She pointed at a blousy off-the-shoulder dress in the window. It was definitely her style.

"Super cute," I said, finding it easier than I'd expected to fall back into our old patterns.

"I'm going to go try it on. Want to come?"

"I think I'll wait out here. I'm enjoying the sunshine."

Cricket smiled. "You need some vitamin D. I'll be right back. Don't go anywhere."

I parked myself on a bench, determined to enjoy my cone and the sweet-tart taste of the passion fruit and ignore everything, including my own grief, for a little while.

I'd made it a whole five minutes before someone cast a shadow over me.

"You sit there like you don't have a care in the world. Disgraceful."

I jerked my head toward the voice coming from beside me and cringed.

*Sylvia Riscoff.*

The last time I'd seen her, she was screaming at me in the emergency room, and that wasn't a moment I wanted to repeat.

I stood and spun around to walk the other way.

"Don't you turn your back on me, girl. You better listen to what I have to say, because I promise you're going to want to hear it."

There was literally nothing I wanted to hear that Sylvia Riscoff could have to say, but that didn't stop me from looking over my shoulder at her. She glared at me, her mouth pinched and brows drawn together.

"That's right. Stop and listen. Because you need to realize that if my son tries to choose you over his family, he's going to regret it for the rest of his life."

I didn't know what she was talking about, and I didn't want to know. I turned and took a step, but she kept talking.

"If he tries to run away with you, his grandfather will cut him off without a dime. He'll lose *everything.*"

I stopped again and turned toward her, still saying nothing. But Sylvia Riscoff didn't need me to speak. She had plenty to say herself.

"You can tell me you don't care. Pretend that you love him, but we both know the truth. His money is the only thing you care about, and if he turns his back on his family to be with a Gable, it will all be *gone.* His birthright will be stripped away. Everything he's been groomed for his entire life. His very *identity* will be forfeit."

The vehemence in her tone took me by surprise, and I stumbled back a step.

"Your mother already killed his father. Only a selfish little whore would take everything else away from him too."

My stomach twisted into a knot as Mrs. Riscoff lifted her chin, stared at me for another moment, and then turned and strode away. She was done with me.

As I watched her disappear around the corner, my mind raced.

*Lincoln knows he'll lose everything if he chooses me, but he still keeps coming.*

I blinked twice, and gelato dripped onto my fingers as a shocking thought occurred to me.

*He must love me like crazy if he's willing to give it all up.*

# LINCOLN

*Present day*

WHITNEY WON'T ANSWER her door or her phone, and she locked the interior door between our rooms. My next choice is either to break in or have someone stand outside her door so she can't leave the hotel without me knowing.

I meant what I said before. I'm not going to lose her again. She needs to know that there is no choice to be made. I already chose her—years ago—and I've never given up.

I'm seconds from kicking in her door when my phone vibrates in my hands, but it's not Whitney.

It's my sister.

"What now?"

"Mother is causing a scene in the lobby, and I'm still ten minutes away. Everyone is afraid to approach her. Please get her out of there."

"Now is not a good time, McKinley."

"It's never a good time to deal with her, but someone has to do it."

"Fuck. Fine. But I'm stealing one of your employees to sit on the VIP floor. Whitney's a flight risk, and I'm not letting that happen."

"Do whatever you need to do, just get to the damn lobby and handle her."

I hang up with my sister and jog down the hall to the bar. After I relieve the bartender of his duties and give him explicit instructions, I head for the elevator.

When I reach the lobby, a crowd has gathered in the atrium area where my mother is spouting off about the Gable whores to anyone who will listen.

*She has officially lost her goddamned mind.* My mother, the queen of *never air your dirty laundry*, is enraged enough to forget every single thing she's ever drilled into me.

I rush toward her and bump into Jackie Gable. She grabs my arm.

"You need to take care of her. I tried to get her to go quietly, but . . . it just went downhill from there."

"I'll take care of it. I'm so sorry you had to hear this."

I march up to my mother and wrap my hand around her upper arm. "You're leaving."

"You chose that whore!"

I pull my mother to the nearest employee-only door and drag her through it. As soon as it closes, she screeches at me.

"Don't you dare drag me around like that! You're my son, and you'll respect me. That whore is ruining you!"

I pull out my phone to call her driver. "Pull around to

the rear employee entrance. My mother will meet you there. You'll return her to the estate, and you won't take her anywhere else for the rest of the night. Understood?"

When I have the affirmative answer I need, I hang up and point toward the rear of the resort. "If you'll follow me, Mother, it's time for you to leave."

The animosity in my mother's glare could peel the paint off walls, but she marches ahead of me, still going off.

"If you think for one second she won't drag you down with her, you're wrong. You'll drag the whole family into the filth surrounding her, and we'll never be clean again. The legacy will be destroyed. All future generations will be tainted."

"You're being melodramatic, Mother. Now tell me—"

"I'll tell you nothing! I won't allow you to do this to us."

"Unfortunately for you, you don't get a say. If you would just let go of your hatred of the Gable family for two seconds, you would realize how ridiculous you're acting."

"That Gable whore murdered my husband. I will *never* forget what happened that night."

Part of me wants to shoot back that he might never have been her legal husband, but I keep that to myself.

When we approach the employee entrance, I try to reason with my mother one more time. "No one will ever forget what happened that night. You can still grieve for your loss. For our loss. But you don't have to place the blame on Whitney. She wasn't there. She had nothing to do with it."

My mother whips around to look at me, anger stamped on her features. "If you think for one moment that Gable women aren't the downfall of Riscoff men, then you haven't been paying attention. All I tried to do was protect you from her. From them. All she wanted was your money, and as soon as she knew you weren't going to get a penny of inheritance from your grandfather, she turned to the arms of another man faster than you could blink. What do you think about that?"

So that's what she told Whitney all those years ago. That I would lose everything if I chose her.

"When did you tell her that?"

"After your father's funeral."

I think back to what happened ten years ago, the events that are burned in my brain. As soon as I piece together the timeline in my head, I know my mother is wrong. *Dead wrong.*

I start laughing.

"Jesus Christ. Now it all makes sense." I shake my head. "You didn't drive her away, Mother. I did that all by myself."

# LINCOLN

*The past*

P*LINK*. The window stayed dark.

I found another small rock and launched it at the window of the upstairs bedroom I knew Whitney was sleeping in. I'd bribed the next-door neighbor's kid who Jackie babysits some nights to get the information. Was I proud of it? No. But I'd do it again.

*Tink.* The pebble connected, but still no light.

I threw another, and finally, a dim glow lit up the room.

*Come on, Blue. I gotta see you. Talk to you. Hold you.*

I tossed another pebble, and it clicked on the window just before the sash slid up. Whitney stuck her head out, her dark hair a cloud around her face.

"Whitney." When I said her name, she looked down at me.

"Lincoln? What are you doing here?"

"Bad impression of Romeo?"

"What do you want?"

"I need to talk to you. Please."

She stared down at me for a few moments before she closed the window and the light went out.

*Fuck. Seriously? She's just going to shut me down like that?*

All this time I'd been telling myself that it was Ricky and Asa and Karma keeping me away from Whitney, but maybe I was wrong.

Maybe she didn't want to see me at all.

Maybe she couldn't get over what happened.

Maybe this was all for nothing . . .

I watched her window for another sign of life, but it didn't come. Frustrated, I jammed my hand into my hair.

"Come on, Blue . . . just give me a chance," I whispered.

"That's what I'm doing, but we have to get out of here."

Whitney's voice came from beside me, scaring the living shit out of me.

"Jesus Christ. I didn't—"

"Where'd you park? We gotta get out of here before someone sees."

She didn't have to tell me twice. I grabbed her hand, and together we jogged down the street to where I parked my truck a block away so no one would see it.

Just having her hand in mine felt so good, I didn't want to let it go. I kept a tight grip on her until I opened the passenger door and helped her in. She was in tiny white pajama shorts, a tank top, no bra, and flip-flops.

*God does exist.*

As soon as I shut her door, I hustled around to my side and jumped in.

"Where can we go that's safe?" she asked. "The cabin?"

When she looked at me, all I wanted to do was drag her across the center console and hold her in my arms.

*Not yet.*

"Yeah. That'll work." As I turned the key, I thought of what happened last time I was there, and how Commodore made me hide out until the black eyes faded, which was yesterday.

I pulled away from the curb and reached out to find Whitney's hand. She grasped mine and kept a tight grip as we drove through town.

We both held our breath as we crossed the bridge where our parents had died. The guardrail had been replaced, and aside from the marks on the pavement, you'd never know it had happened.

"I'm so sorry about your dad." She spoke so quietly that I barely heard her say it as we cleared the other side of the bridge. "Really sorry. I can't believe . . ." Her voice broke.

"I know. It's not your fault. None of it. I'm so fucking sorry about your parents. I'm sorry about every single fucking bit of it. That I didn't listen to you about Ricky. That we fought. For what my mother said at the hospital. All of it." I looked over at Whitney in the passenger seat, and the street lights illuminated her stricken face every few seconds. "Please don't cry, Blue. Please."

"It still doesn't feel real, does it? I mean . . . if I try to forget the funeral, sometimes I can almost convince myself that I just haven't seen my parents in a couple weeks, and they'll walk through the door anytime. It doesn't feel like they're gone forever. Like I'll never get to see them again."

I couldn't stop the tears tracking down her face, but I did feel every bit of the anguish in her tone and understood exactly what she meant. "I get it. It's like my dad is on an overseas business trip and is ignoring the fact he has a family."

"Why does it have to be real? Why do so many bad things have to happen? And why—"

I didn't know what other question she was going to ask, but she cut herself off.

"What?"

"Nothing. I don't want to think about it tonight. I don't really want to think about any of it. That's all I do, is think about it. I'm so tired of feeling broken."

I squeezed her hand harder as we turned down the gravel drive that led to the cabin, and I parked. "Let me help put you back together, Blue. That's all I want."

I helped her out of the truck and kept her pressed tightly to my side as we entered the cabin. As soon as the door closed, I wrapped my arms around her and held her against my chest. I rested my chin on her head, and together we stood there in silence.

"I'm so sorry. So fucking sorry."

Her body shook, and I rocked her from side to side until she finally looked up at me. "I didn't know how much I needed that until right now."

I threaded my fingers into her hair and cradled the back of her head. "I'll help you any way I can, Blue. All you have to do is tell me what you need."

Her arms wrapped around my neck.

"You. I need you."

# WHITNEY

I'D BEEN DROWNING in grief for what seemed like a million years, sleepwalking through every minute of every day, but as soon as Lincoln wrapped his arms around me, it was like I snapped awake.

"I don't want to talk about what happened," I told him. "I don't want to think about it. I don't want to drown anymore."

"You don't have to do anything you don't want. I've got you. I won't let you go until you tell me to."

*I never want him to let me go.*

I pulled Lincoln's head down to mine and took control of the kiss. Power flooded my veins, and I finally felt like I had control over *something* in my life. It was a heady illusion, but I was going to take every bit of it I could get.

"Blue—" He said my nickname against my lips, but I wasn't stopping.

"Just kiss me."

"Whatever you want. Tonight's all about you."

He bent his knees, slid an arm under my legs, and picked me up. I gripped the muscles of his shoulders and they flexed and hardened.

Just the simple act of having my hands on him reminded me that I was *alive*. I hadn't felt alive since they told me my parents were gone.

*No. Not thinking about that.*

Lincoln laid me on the bed, and I snagged the hem of his shirt before he could step away.

"Off. Take it off."

He didn't question me, just whipped the shirt over his head.

"I don't want sweet or soft. I want . . ." My words trailed off because I didn't know how to express what I needed. "I want to feel alive."

A wave of emotion flashed across Lincoln's face, but it was gone before I could identify it.

"I know. I need that too."

I sat up and reached for the button on his jeans, flipping it free and letting them fall. When he was standing naked before me, the sight was enough to block any coherent thought from my brain other than *this feels right.*

He stepped forward, and I reached for him as he slipped my straps off my shoulders. "I've missed you so fucking much."

"Hurry." I shimmied out of my shorts and tossed my tank over my head.

Thoughts of how it was the last time we were here and how it ended start to invade my brain, and I had to block them out. I bolted up to my knees and threw myself at him, my chest against his, my hands tangling in the ends of his hair.

It was like flipping a switch on Lincoln. His hands clutched my shoulders and then one dropped to my ass. I bucked my hips against him, trapping his cock between us.

"God, Blue."

"Stop talking to God and take me."

I dropped to my butt and spread my legs wide, pulling him between them.

"We need—"

"I don't care right now. I just need to feel this and forget everything else."

Lincoln's expression hardened as if he was fighting a battle with himself, and clearly, I lost. He didn't push inside me, bare, the way I expected. No, he dropped to his knees and his mouth found my center. His tongue swept my lips apart, lashing me over and over as he teased my clit. My hips lifted, and he used one hand to hold me down as the other circled a finger around my entrance.

"You want me here." He pushed in to the first knuckle before pulling free.

"Yes."

His fingers slid inside, but it wasn't his fingers I wanted. But the pleasure assaulted my senses, and I let it build. Blood pounded in my ears, drowning out my own moans as he added another finger. His lips latched onto my clit and he sucked, tripping me over the edge to orgasm. My inner muscles clamped down on his fingers as I came.

"Fuck, Blue. *Fuck.*"

He pulled free and seconds later, I was full again, but

this time his cock stretched me wide as he pounded into me.

"Yes. Yes. Like that."

He went harder and faster, and I lost track of everything except for how he lit my body up. The orgasm hit me harder than ever before, and everything inside me, including all the pieces that were already broken, shattered into dust as I screamed.

"I love you!"

There was no way he could miss the words. Lincoln stilled, and I felt his cock pump into me.

"Shit. I was going to pull out. I meant to, but it—"

"It's okay. I'm on the pill. We're fine."

I hoped he was too worried about that to bring up what I'd said. *Why did I say it?* Because I wanted to feel something other than sorrow and loss?

"Blue—"

"Can you get me a washcloth? I need to clean up."

Lincoln nodded slowly and pulled out. His gaze lingered on me before he walked to the bathroom, and I heard running water. When he reappeared a minute later, he held out a towel and I took it from him.

"You know I would take care of you if it wasn't fine."

My head jerked up at his words. "What?"

Lincoln looked down at me, his expression soft. "I want to take care of you, regardless. You don't have to live in your aunt's house, sharing a room with your cousin. I can get you your own place. Then we won't have to keep coming here." He waved an arm toward the bed. "We'd have privacy. Away from everyone. No one could interrupt us."

"What are you saying?" I blinked again, and then twice more as I stared at him.

"I want to take care of you, Whitney. Let me."

For a few precious minutes, I'd gotten to shut the world out, but now everything came roaring back.

"You want to *take care of me*? Like . . . pay for me to have a place to live?" I was so shocked by what he was saying, I had to make sure that I wasn't misunderstanding.

"Yeah. And your bills. Get you a car. You could go to school, if you want. I'll make sure your tuition is covered too."

A greasy feeling pooled in my stomach, and I snatched up the sheet and pulled it over me.

"*Tuition*?" I felt like a parrot, repeating everything he said.

"Yeah. Spending money, whatever you need."

I blinked a few more times, waiting for him to start laughing and tell me it was a joke, but he didn't.

I clutched the sheet to my chest. "You want to give me an allowance?"

Some of Lincoln's earnest expression faded away. "Not like an allowance, but . . . I just don't want you to have to worry about money."

I shook my head, my mouth hanging open. "And we'll keep seeing each other. You paying all my bills . . ."

"Well, yeah." Lincoln looked confused.

"So you want me to be your side piece tucked up in some house in town. A convenient spot for you to stop and get your rocks off before you go home to the estate and whichever socialite your mom picks out for you?" I jumped off the bed and snagged my clothes from the floor.

"Whitney, you're making it sound—"

"Like you want me to be your whore? Because that's exactly what it sounds like to me!" I yanked the tank over my head and tugged on my shorts.

Lincoln jammed his hands into his hair. "Not like that. I just want you to have everything you need and not have to work or worry about money."

I coughed and laughed at the same time. "And what would you tell your mom when she found out and had another heart attack?"

"She doesn't have to know—"

My laughter came harsher and louder. "Yeah, that's what I thought. Like father, like son. Not fucking happening."

I marched toward the door to the bedroom as he struggled to get his jeans on. *Not a fucking chance, Lincoln Riscoff. I won't be your whore.*

This time, as I walked through the living room, I was smart enough to snag the keys from the table where Lincoln had left them.

"Whitney, wait! That's not—"

"No. I'm done waiting for you to man up, Lincoln. I'm *done with all of this.*" I slammed the door on my way out. "You can't buy me!"

I hoped he liked walking home this time.

# LINCOLN

*Present day*

MY MOTHER HAD LAID the seeds of doubt in Whitney's mind, and I'd played right into them the night I finally got to see her. I was young and stupid then, and all I knew was that I'd never felt like that about anyone before Whitney Gable.

I didn't realize I'd never feel that way about anyone else, but I won't be making the same mistake again.

As soon as my mother is in the back of an SUV and on her way to the estate, I return to the front desk to make myself a key card for Whitney's room. She and I are going to talk tonight whether she wants to or not.

Jackie Gable, who should be long since off shift, stands in front of the computer when I step behind the counter.

*Fuck.* It didn't even occur to me to wonder why she

was still in her uniform in the lobby when she tried to deal with my mother, because my brain was otherwise occupied.

"You're working late."

"Someone called in sick, and it was easy enough for me to cover the shift."

"We appreciate it," I say as I glance at the machine used to make key cards.

Jackie's gaze follows mine. I've never thought she was an idiot, and it doesn't take her long to guess why I'm here.

She shakes her head at me. "Please tell me you're not here for the reason I think you are."

"I need a key made."

"I know that I have absolutely no grounds to refuse to do this for you, but I'm refusing all the same. If my niece doesn't want to see you, you can't make her."

I straighten and meet Jackie's gaze, a paler blue version of Whitney's. "Then you can move out of the way and I'll do it myself. I'm not asking your permission, Ms. Gable."

Jackie's jaw tenses and I can tell she wants to tell me to go to hell, but she steps aside instead. Her professional demeanor slips as I take her place. "You better be really damn sure—"

I turn to pierce her with my stare. "Do you want your niece leaving town in the morning because of what my mother said to her tonight?"

Jackie stiffens. "What did she say?"

"I'm sure you can guess, given what you heard in the

lobby earlier. Now, I need a damn key so I can fix this before she disappears from my life for another ten years."

Jackie shoves me out of the way. "I'll do it. I guarantee I'm faster."

# WHITNEY

I STARE out at the darkness. The only thing I can hear from where I'm curled up on the terrace is the rushing water of the river below.

*Tonight will be the last night I hear the river. Tomorrow, I'm gone.*

I wrap the blanket tighter around my shoulders and think about how the hell I'm going to make this up to Cricket. She'll be devastated. But in the end, I think she'll understand.

*I hope she understands.*

From behind me comes a whooshing sound, and I jerk around to see a form step out into the darkness from my room. I open my mouth to scream, but he turns on the light.

*Lincoln.*

"How did you get in here?"

He holds up the plastic card. "Your aunt made me a key."

*The traitor*. Although, she probably has no idea what happened tonight.

"She shouldn't have. It's not going to make this any easier."

"Yeah, it is. Because you're not going anywhere, Blue. Not this time."

Tears burn in my eyes again. "You only get one mother, Lincoln. You can't choose—"

He shakes his head and comes around to crouch in front of me. "There's no choice to be made. That's been done for years. I was too young and stupid to realize it before, but I'm not now. She told me what she said to you. How she tried to scare you, and then I fed into all of it that night at the cabin and pushed you away." His hands cup the sides of my face, and he looks into my eyes. "I'm never pushing you away again."

I know what Lincoln's thinking right now. If he chooses me over his mother, we can live happily ever after, and I wish that were true. But there's no way I can ever be happy knowing I caused that breach with his family. He may think his mother will get over it, but I know the truth. That woman will hate me until the day she dies, and I won't be responsible for causing that break.

I wasn't lying when I said that there's nothing I wouldn't do to see my mom again. To hear her voice. To smell her perfume. To listen to her hum as she cleaned the house.

*Nothing.*

"Please tell me you believe me, Blue."

That's the only easy part of this whole situation. "Of course I believe you," I tell him.

"And you forgive me?"

This life has taught me more than anything that holding on to a grudge is the biggest mistake of all. I don't know what he really thinks he needs forgiveness for, but I'm not holding on to any of it.

"I forgive you."

His mouth finds mine, and every emotion comes through his kiss. Pain, regret, loss, sorrow. I taste them on my lips, and they make the kiss even more bittersweet.

No matter what Lincoln wants, tonight is good-bye.

One last night.

Maybe it's unfair for me to take it, but it'll be the memory I hold on to when I'm sleeping alone and missing him.

# LINCOLN

I CARRY WHITNEY INSIDE, and as soon as I set her down, her fingers tear at the buttons of my shirt. The thread gives way, and they go flying.

*She wants me just as badly as I want her.* That's how it's always been. She's always matched me kiss for kiss, touch for touch, thrust for thrust.

Tonight, I want to savor her, but she's rushing, almost desperate to strip us both naked.

*I will never not give her what she wants. Never again.*

Her robe falls to the floor, revealing her naked curves.

"So fucking beautiful."

She backs up until her shoulders press against the slider, and she uses the leverage to wrap first one leg around my hip and then the other.

"You sure this is what you want?"

"Yes. I don't want to forget this."

"I can give you unforgettable."

I grip her hips, holding her against the door as I pull

back a few inches to fit my cock against her. I open my mouth to ask her if she's ready, but she's already soaked.

"You're always ready for me."

"I can't help it. I've wanted you all night."

"I always want to give you what you want."

With my gaze locked on hers, I push inside her inch by inch, watching her pupils dilate and her bottom lip fall open.

"I love watching you. So sexy. So incredible."

Her hips buck against me. "Faster."

"I need you on the bed to do this right." I pull her off the glass, my hands cupping her ass as I walk to the edge of the bed. Instead of laying her down on her back, I sit, and she kneels above me.

"Take what you need."

Whitney nods, and she starts to move. I let her set the pace, control every single thing, and she looks fucking magnificent as her head tips back and her black hair swings free.

She pushes at my shoulders and I lie back, shoving us further toward the middle of the bed. Whitney goes wild, her hips bucking and grinding, and she says my name over and over.

I reach out and find her clit with my thumb.

"Oh God. Yes. Yes. Like that."

Whitney picks up the pace and before long, I'm the one yelling her name as I lose control and empty myself inside her.

# WHITNEY

I NEVER WANT TO MOVE. Ever.

Lincoln sleeps beside me on his stomach, his arm stretched out and his hand on my belly. My gaze drifts between his fingers and the sun rising over the gorge.

With each passing moment, I know the clock is ticking down. My bags are packed and waiting in the living room. My outfit for today is folded on the chair, just waiting for me to dress and walk out of The Gables and Lincoln Riscoff's life forever.

When the room is bathed in yellow, I know I can't put it off any longer. It's time.

I roll out from under his hand, grab my clothes, and sneak into the bathroom. I wash my face, swipe on just enough makeup to get by, dress, and open the door just as silently as I entered.

I tiptoe out into the bedroom, but the bed is empty. Lincoln's gone.

*Did he run when he had the chance?*

I walk into the living room and find him standing by the door, his arms crossed.

"What the hell is this?" He jerks his head toward my suitcases.

I swallow. "I told you. I have to go."

"And last night? What the fuck was that?"

"Good-bye," I say, a hint of shame wrapping around me.

Lincoln shakes his head. "No. No more fucking good-byes. You leave? I leave. That's how this works, Blue."

"You can't. You have a life here. A family that loves you—"

"And so do you."

The man is impossible. I look up at the ceiling, find my confidence, and stare him down again. "I can't stay here and drive a wedge between you and your mother. I won't."

Lincoln's hard expression doesn't shift. "And I'm done letting other people manipulate our lives to keep us apart. I'm fucking done. You leave, I leave. End of story."

"I'm not worth it." My voice breaks on the last word.

Lincoln's arms fall to his sides. "Bullshit." He strides toward me, his hands going out to cup my cheeks. "You're worth everything. *Every-fucking-thing.* I have fucked up over and over again when it comes to you, and I'm not doing it again. I felt it last night. You felt it too."

My lip trembles. "I told you, that was good-bye."

"No, it wasn't." He looks at my suitcases. "You need to get out of Gable? You need to get out of this fucking hotel and away from this madness? I can do that. I *will* do that."

He releases my cheeks and whips out his phone, tapping the screen a few times before lifting it to his ear.

"Fuel up the chopper. I want it on the helipad at The Gables in thirty minutes or less. I'm going to Blue House."

"What are you doing?"

Lincoln smiles. "Getting us both the hell out of here. I told you . . . you leave, I leave."

"Lincoln!"

He shakes his head, and I recognize the stubborn look on his face. "You're not getting rid of me this time, Blue. Not a fucking chance. We're in this together. Whatever comes next, we face it *together*."

I swallow because I love the sound of that. I want it to be that easy.

*But nothing ever is.*

# WHITNEY

*The past*

WHEN I WALKED downstairs at Jackie's house the next morning, the only thing I could think was *at least I didn't let him throw me out again.* I took a stand. I could still respect myself this morning, even if I felt like my heart was breaking all over again.

Maybe there was some way it could work between us . . . *somehow?*

I walked into the living room on my way to the kitchen and froze.

"Hey, baby," Ricky said as he jumped up from the couch.

My eyes must have been as wide as dinner plates as they tracked from him to Aunt Jackie, Asa, Cricket, Karma, and *Ricky's mom* all in the room. Cricket's face looked strained, and she shook her head like she was trying to send me a message.

*What the hell is going on here?*

"Are you okay?" Asa asked. "Sleeping till noon isn't normally your thing. And does anyone know whose truck is parked out front?"

*Oh shit.* It didn't even occur to me that I needed to park Lincoln's truck farther away from the house, because I was too upset.

"I swear I've seen that truck before," Karma said, and the keys hung like dead weight in my hoodie pocket.

"I need coffee," I blurted, poised to escape to the kitchen.

Ricky stepped forward. "Not yet. I have something I need to ask you first."

"Can it wait until—" My question trailed off as he dropped on one knee, right there in Aunt Jackie's living room in front of both our families.

*Oh my God. Oh my God. No. This isn't happening.*

Blood rushed in my ears, practically drowning out the words he said next.

"Baby, you know I need you more than I've ever needed anyone in my life. I want to take care of you. Take you away from here. After this summer and everything that's happened, I realized that life is too short to take chances. So I have to do this now. Marry me, Whitney."

Hot tears slid down my cheeks. "I can't do this right now. I can't." My voice shook, but my feet came unglued from where they'd been stuck to the floor.

I spun around and bolted for the front door. It crashed shut behind me, and I ran barefoot across the lawn.

My brain was a roiling mess, and the only thought that made any sense was *get out of here.*

I fished the keys out of my pocket and dropped them twice on the ground as I rushed to the truck. I didn't even care that my brother was going to grill me about whose truck it was later. I just had to leave. *Now.*

As soon as I climbed inside, the passenger door flew open. My head jerked to the side.

It wasn't Ricky.

No, it was his mom, her face pinched and angry. "I knew . . . I knew when I saw this truck."

My entire body started to shake at her words.

"You think I wouldn't recognize it? It's the same type of truck the groundskeepers use at the Riscoff estate, and the same as what Roosevelt Riscoff used to drive when he came to see *me.*"

My head jerked back against the seat, hitting it hard enough it bounced. *"What?"* I gasped out the word. "You—"

Renee Rango's gaze narrowed on me. "Don't you dare judge me. You don't know anything. But I do. I know exactly what's going to happen if you keep trying to reach for something that's so high above you. You think that boy will ever give you the life you want? No way. He'll hide you away just like his father hid me until he pays you off to stay quiet about it ever happening."

"Oh my God," I whispered.

She nodded. "Yes, I've been where you are. I was stupid then. Naive. Trusting. I thought he loved me, and that eventually he'd find a way to tell his father that he wanted to be with me, no matter my background." She laughed, and bitterness dripped from the sound. "Well, that didn't happen. You don't have the bloodlines they want either."

Everything she said compounded on what Lincoln had said last night, and the greasy feeling plaguing me since then grew.

"He paid you off?"

Her lips twisted into an ugly smile. "Because I thought I was so smart. I got him to take me to Vegas. We had a quickie wedding he didn't even remember because he was hammered. I didn't bother to show him the marriage license until I had a positive pregnancy test in hand. I thought I had him by the balls then."

I blinked twice, unable to believe what I was hearing. *A pregnancy test? Did that mean Ricky was . . .* I couldn't even finish the thought before Renee kept going.

"And you know what he didn't do? He didn't take me home to Daddy to tell him he was going to be a grandpa. No, he hired some shyster of an attorney to divorce me, paid me off, and threatened to take my baby from me and make it so he was raised by people so far away that I'd never find him again. If you think for one second they wouldn't do the same to you—or worse—then you're dumber than I thought you were."

*Oh my God.* I knew Lincoln's father wasn't a great man, but that seemed awfully cruel. "I don't know what to say . . ." I stared down at my hands curled into my lap, squeezing them tight to stop the shaking.

"All you need to do is march your ass back into that house and tell my son you're going to marry him."

I jerked my head up to look at her. "What?"

Her lips pinched together. "You heard me. You're going to marry my son."

"But I don't love him. You know I don't. You can't possibly want me to marry him."

She lifted her chin. "I don't give one good goddamn what you feel or don't. My son needs you. He told me you write all his songs and that without you, he can't be the rock star he wants to be. I've sacrificed everything to make my boy happy, and I'm not about to let some girl spreading her legs for a Riscoff ruin it."

"You're insane."

Renee shook her head slowly. "No, I'm a mother. And when your mom left Roosevelt Riscoff to die in that river, she took my paycheck with her. If you don't marry my son and make him into a goddamned rock star, you'll leave me with only one choice."

"What?"

That ugly smile twisted her lips again. "I'll go public. I'll destroy your little boyfriend's family and tell them all exactly who my son is—the legitimate heir to the Riscoff fortune."

My entire body tensed with shock. *Ricky is Lincoln's half brother. His* older *half brother*.

The entire town knew about the Riscoff inheritance tradition. Everything went to the oldest male of the next generation. Which meant . . . *if I don't marry Ricky, Lincoln will get nothing*.

"I see you get what I'm saying."

My mind spun in a million different directions at the same time, and my heart clenched painfully. "But you could've done that already. Could do that at any time. Why should I believe that you wouldn't anyway?"

Renee's green eyes pierced me, and for the first time, I realized that she wasn't all there. I didn't know if it was what happened with Lincoln's father that broke her, but Ricky's mom was crazy.

"My boy doesn't want to be a Riscoff. He wants to be a rock star. And Ricky always gets what he wants, which includes *you*. You're going to marry him and help him live that dream of his . . . or I'll make sure he takes every single penny that's supposed to go to your boyfriend."

The woman was unhinged. Absolutely, totally, and completely. But I knew with complete certainty that she was also deadly serious.

The other thing I knew with complete certainty? If Ricky were to inherit the Riscoff fortune, he'd piss away every penny chasing his rock star dream. He'd run the companies into the ground because he wouldn't give a single damn about how many people relied on the Riscoff name for a paycheck.

Ricky would ruin this entire town. That was the reason I gave myself for the sickening realization that I had to do what Renee said. But the truth lay just beneath the surface, and even my pride wasn't enough to keep it quiet.

*I love Lincoln too much to let Ricky and Renee destroy everything that matters to him.*

He'd never marry me, and I wouldn't be his kept woman. *But I can save his future.*

Renee must have seen the decision on my face, because she smiled sweetly. "I knew you'd see it my way. Now, here comes my son. You better make it convincing."

Feeling like my body was suddenly that of a ninety-year-old woman, I climbed out of the truck. Ricky stood in the front yard, staring at me.

"Baby, please don't go. I know you want out of this town as bad as I do. I'll take care of you, I promise."

I thought I'd felt sick when Lincoln said those same words to me, but that was only because I hadn't heard them from Ricky's lips while I was being forced into something I didn't want. Now they were a hundred times worse.

I looked at Renee over my shoulder, and she nodded with a manic smile on her face.

*She's completely crazy.* Which meant I had no choice. I couldn't let her carry through with her threats. For the first time in my life, I was going to do something noble and worthy.

Ricky came toward me, holding out the ring. "Marry me, Whitney. Please."

All the nobility in the world couldn't stop my stomach from roiling as I forced myself to say the word that was going to change the rest of my life.

"Yes."

# LINCOLN

*Present day*

THE BELLMAN TAKES Whitney's luggage up to the helipad before I lead her out of the room.

"Lincoln! Come join us!"

I hear my mother's voice coming from the lounge at the end of the VIP hall near the bar. She's sitting at a table eating breakfast with Maren Higgins.

*How the fuck did she get up here again?*

Whitney steps out beside me.

"Mother, I told you—"

My mother stands, and Whitney stiffens beside me.

"You don't need that whore," my mother snaps. "Not when you have Maren—"

"Give it a rest, Sylvia." Jackie steps out of her suite and walks toward my mother. She stops beside her table. "Haven't we all lost enough? Isn't it time to finally bury the ax? If they want to be together, let them."

*Finally, someone who has some goddamned sense.*

"You might work for my daughter, but you can't speak to me that way."

"And I'm not going to let you treat my niece like this. She's never done a thing to you, so why don't you just let them be *happy*."

My phone buzzes in my pocket, and I pull it out. It's the pilot. He's arrived.

"We're leaving, Mother. We'll be back when the media circus dies down. I suggest you take a vacation and do the same."

I slide my fingers into Whitney's and lead her down the hall in the opposite direction.

"You little whore! You're just like your mother! I won't let you—"

"For the love of God, shut up, Sylvia."

Thankfully, my mother finally listens to Jackie and goes silent.

Whitney stops and looks at me, indecision clear on her face. "Are you sure about this?"

"I've never been more sure of anything in my life." I squeeze her hand. "I love you."

Whitney's blue eyes shine. "I love you too."

"Then let's get the hell out of here."

I lead her toward the stairs that will take us to the heli-pad. I'm tempted to look over my shoulder, to see the shock on my mother's face that I'm not caving to her demands, but I have no desire to look backward.

Today is all about moving forward—to my future with Whitney.

I HAVE no idea how long we've been in the chopper, and I still have no idea where we're going other than it's called Blue House. I don't exactly want to presume about the significance of the name either. Honestly, right now, it doesn't matter to me where we go.

*Lincoln loves me.*

I try to use that to salve the ache in my heart over the rift I've caused between him and his mother.

*I will find a way to fix it,* I promise myself. Only then can I allow myself to smile and feel the joy surging in my soul.

*Lincoln loves me.*

He squeezes my hand from the seat beside me as we fly toward the ocean and dozens of islands. I open my mouth to ask where we're going, but he speaks first.

"I hope you like whale watching, because the view of the straits of San Juan is incredible from the house."

"You own a house in Washington?"

238

He smiles wider. "I own an island in Washington. The house is totally self-sufficient. Impossible for the press to get to unless they have a boat or a chopper."

"Of course you own a freaking island." I can't stop myself from laughing. "It sounds like paradise."

"It is, and we'll be there in about thirty minutes."

"You didn't pack anything."

"I have all I need already there. It's where I go when I need to get away from everything and everyone. You're going to love it. No venues. No hotel rooms. Just experiences you'll never forget."

Lincoln's phone vibrates between us, but he shoves it in his pocket without looking at it.

I lose myself in the view of the ocean and the islands. Completely breathtaking.

True to his word, we touch down on a helipad a half hour later, and my phone vibrates in my purse. I pull it out and see several missed calls and text notifications.

Lincoln pulls out his phone when it vibrates again. "Sometimes I wish this place didn't have cell service," he says, glancing down at his phone. "It's my brother. I don't even want to answer it."

"My aunt called three times." I lift my gaze to Lincoln, and a horrible premonition washes over me. "Maybe you should answer it."

Lincoln's expression turns grim as he taps the screen to accept the call on speakerphone. "What do you need, Harrison?"

"You finally did it. You fucking killed her."

Lincoln's face pales. "What the fuck are you talking about?"

"Mother was pronounced dead at the hospital a half hour ago. Heart attack. They couldn't resuscitate her. You fucking killed her. I hope you're happy."

---

*Whitney and Lincoln's story will conclude in Reveling in Sin.*

*Beneath These Shadows*

*Beneath The Truth*

DIRTY BILLIONAIRE TRILOGY:

*Dirty Billionaire*

*Dirty Pleasures*

*Dirty Together*

DIRTY GIRL DUET:

*Dirty Girl*

*Dirty Love*

REAL DUET:

*Real Good Man*

*Real Good Love*

REAL DIRTY DUET:

*Real Dirty*

*Real Sexy*

FLASH BANG SERIES:

*Flash Bang*

*Hard Charger*

STANDALONES:

*Take Me Back*

*Bad Judgment*

# ABOUT THE AUTHOR

Meghan March has been known to wear camo face paint and tromp around in the woods wearing mud-covered boots, all while sporting a perfect manicure. She's also impulsive, easily entertained, and absolutely unapologetic about the fact that she loves to read and write smut.

Her past lives include slinging auto parts, selling lingerie, making custom jewelry, and practicing corporate law. Writing books about dirty-talking alpha males and the strong, sassy women who bring them to their knees is by far the most fabulous job she's ever had.

She would love to hear from you. Connect with her at:

Website:
www.meghanmarch.com
Facebook:
www.facebook.com/MeghanMarchAuthor
Twitter:

www.twitter.com/meghan_march
Instagram:
www.instagram.com/meghanmarch

98628991R00154

Made in the USA
Middletown, DE
09 November 2018